Praise for *The Dese*

CW01511688

'You won't be disappointed!'
LostCousins

'Nathan's concise yet evocative writing style makes every page a pleasure to read. The characters come alive, and the historical backdrop enriches the storytelling. Whether you're a genealogy enthusiast or simply love a well-crafted mystery, *The Deserter's Tale* delivers'
Cheshire Ancestor

'The writing is easy and fast paced, intriguing, mysterious, and often humorous. Every genealogy researcher can relate to the great research tips and methodology that the author describes'
The London Leaf

'The past and the present are interwoven with skill, the family history research is described with consummate precision and realism'
Waltham Forest Family History Society

'Nathan has once again demonstrated his skill in excellent creative writing, providing an intriguing story to the very end'
Hampshire Genealogical Society

'Nathan Dylan Goodwin does a great job of creating a plot that keeps you reading, wanting answers and more of Morton's adventures'
Gwent Family History Society

'If you have any interest in genealogy and good mysteries, you will thoroughly enjoy these well-crafted tales'
Columbia Historical & Genealogical Society

About the Author

Nathan Dylan Goodwin is a writer, genealogist and educator. He was born and raised in Hastings, East Sussex. Having attended school in the town, he then completed a Bachelor of Arts degree in Radio, Film and Television Studies, followed by a Master of Arts degree in Creative Writing at Canterbury Christ Church University. A member of the Society of Authors and the Crime Writers' Association, he has completed several local history books about Hastings, as well as several works of fiction, including the acclaimed *Forensic Genealogist* series, the *Mrs McDougall Investigates* series and the *Venator Cold Case* series. His other interests include theatre, reading, running, skiing, travelling and, of course, genealogy. He is a qualified teacher, member of the Guild of One-Name Studies and the Society of Genealogists, as well as being a member of the Sussex Family History Group, the Norfolk Family History Society and the Kent Family History Society. He lives in Kent with his husband, son, dog and an assortment of chickens.

NathanDylanGoodwin

By the same author

nonfiction:
Hastings at War 1939-1945
Hastings Wartime Memories and Photographs
Hastings & St Leonards Through Time
Around Battle Through Time

fiction:
(The Forensic Genealogist series)
The Asylum - A Morton Farrier short story
Hiding the Past
The Lost Ancestor
The Orange Lilies – A Morton Farrier novella
The America Ground
The Spyglass File
The Missing Man – A Morton Farrier novella
The Suffragette's Secret – A Morton Farrier short story
The Wicked Trade
The Sterling Affair
The Foundlings
The Deserter's Tale – A Morton Farrier novella

(The Mrs McDougall Investigates series)
Ghost Swifts, Blue Poppies and the Red Star

(Venator Cold Case series)
The Chester Creek Murders
The Sawtooth Slayer
The Hollywood Strangler

The Deserter's Tale
by
Nathan Dylan Goodwin

Cover design: Patrick Dengate
Original image from the Ferron and Bracken Photograph Collection, Special Collections and Archives, University Libraries, University of Nevada, Las Vegas.

To my husband, Robert John Bristow
Thanks for so willingly joining the adventure

Chapter One

25th February 2023, Rye, East Sussex

Morton Farrier was flustered. He was sitting at the kitchen table of his beloved fifteenth-century home, The House with Two Front Doors on Rye's historic Mermaid Street, trying—and generally failing—to finish a PowerPoint presentation. From the next room, his son, Isaac, was smashing the merry hell out of a drum kit, which Morton's mother-in-law had thoughtfully bought for his third birthday last week. Despite Morton and his wife, Juliette, showering Isaac with a variety of gifts, his outright favourite present of all had been the wretched, deafening drum kit.

'Isaac!' Morton shouted into the lounge.

Isaac paused mid-thrashing. 'Yes, Daddy?'

'Do you think you could play with something else, now? Daddy's getting a headache.'

'One more song,' Isaac replied, resuming his drumming.

'If only it *was* a song,' Morton muttered, standing up and walking across the hallway to the lounge. He saw his almost-six-year-old daughter, Grace, somehow managing to read a book on the sofa behind the monstrous drum kit that now dominated the family living room. 'How on earth are you able to concentrate on reading?' he asked her.

Grace glanced up at him as if he were the greater distraction, shrugged and carried on with her book.

Morton winced as Isaac launched into a frenzied phase of the drumming session, which instantly put him in mind of Animal from *The Muppet Show*. Not for the first time, he watched on, contemplating with slight astonishment that he had spawned such a creature as this. He hurried from the room, headed up to his study on the top floor of the house and put

1

his noise-cancelling earbuds in, sighing with relief as his world fell into near-silence.

He headed back down to the kitchen, beelining for his only ally in the home: the coffee machine. But, as he went to switch it on, he caught sight of an open bottle of Diablo red wine at the end of the worktop and promptly poured himself a glass of that instead.

'Right,' he said to himself, sipping the wine as he sat down at his laptop. 'Where was I?' He was a long way from finished; that was where he was. He was due to give a talk, entitled *Researching Your Sussex Ancestors* at RootsTech, the international genealogy conference in Salt Lake City, Utah, in just five days' time but he was nowhere near organised or ready. On top of his unfinished presentation, yesterday Morton had been asked to fill-in for a last-minute presenter drop-out. He had somehow agreed to deliver a twenty-minute case-study relevant to genetic genealogy as part of a panel of DNA experts, incorporating the theme of family. Now that he was thinking about it, he had no idea what his presentation would be about. He'd certainly worked on several cases where genetic genealogy had played a pivotal role in their resolution; but which of them to pick?

Morton carried his glass of wine over to the window, his mind raking back through all the cases that he had worked on over the past few years. He gazed out over the narrow, cobbled Mermaid Street, which was devoid of its usual tourists, owing to the inclement weather.

He considered the potential of one recent case, where he had used DNA to help unpick a complicated spy story that had dated back to the 1950s Suez Crisis. It was certainly an interesting enough case but one which he was fairly sure would be impossible to boil down into a coherent twenty-minute presentation: it would need a whole book to fully explore its complexities.

He drank more wine and gazed on up the street, thinking about his own complicated story and whether that might just fit the bill. Personal journeys were always a winner at these events. At the age of fifteen, Morton's father had clumsily informed him of the fact that he had been adopted as a baby, creating a deep disconnect between his past and present with which he had only recently begun to come to terms. The past ten years had been a journey of discovery, first finding the identity of his biological mother and then his biological father, the latter having known nothing of his existence. DNA tests across all the major genealogy companies had greatly supplemented his own genealogical research, adding new family members and revealing long-forgotten secrets in the process. But, in this instance, genetic genealogy had not provided the most crucial pieces of the puzzle; so, it didn't quite fit the bill for the presentation.

As his thoughts moved on to another case which might be relevant, his mother-in-law, Margot, entered his field of vision. She was walking up the street and approaching the house, laden with a variety of shopping bags.

Morton quickly downed the wine, rushed the glass over to the sink and just managed to sit back down at his laptop as she entered the house. He glanced up as she waltzed into the kitchen. 'Oh, hi, Margot,' he said casually.

Margot smiled as she placed her bags down on the stone floor with a sigh. 'It's a bit early for wine, isn't it?'

'Sorry?' Morton said, removing his earbuds but having obviously heard what she had just said.

'I said that it's a bit early for wine,' she repeated.

'Er,' he began, scrabbling about in his mind for how to respond to her.

'Hi, Granny,' Grace said, entering the kitchen and saving Morton from having to justify drinking wine at… What *was* the time, anyway? He looked at the clock at the top of his computer: *10:54.* Maybe it *was* perhaps a little too early.

Margot pulled Grace into a hug. 'Hello, my darling.' She inclined her head towards the racket coming from the lounge.

3

'He does love that drum kit, doesn't he? It is *so* good for him to have a musical interest at this age.'

'Hmm,' Morton muttered, not sure that anyone within a five-mile radius of the house would agree with her. 'Have you had a good morning?' he asked Margot, keen to change the subject away from drumming and his early drinking.

'Yes. Lovely, thank you. Listen, don't tell your brother, but I had brunch at The Fig. A Mushroom Benny and a latte. Delicious. I went to Granny's Scones before, fully intending to eat there—of course—but when I saw the scone of the day in the window... Well, I was rather put off eating at all, to be quite frank. Then, I saw The Fig out of the corner of my eye and sneakily backed away. And, well, I went there instead.'

'I'm not sure I dare enquire what the scone of the day was...' Morton said with a grimace. His adopted brother, Jeremy, ran a small, quirky scone shop on Rye High Street with his husband, Guy. They sold some great food, but occasionally the flavours of the scones left much to be desired.

'Hey, let me guess!' Grace shrieked, enthusiastically jumping up and down. 'Worm and cauliflower?'

Morton laughed. 'Tadpole and custard?'

Margot raised her eyebrows. 'Mint and parmesan.'

'Yuk,' Grace concluded.

'Yesterday it was beetroot and tuna,' Morton informed them.

'Honestly. I'm always surprised they can get any customers at all with these outlandish concoctions of theirs,' Margot said, rifling in one of the shopping bags. She pulled out a stack of paperbacks and held them up gleefully in front of Morton. 'Got these from the Ethel Loves Me shop. They'll keep me going for the few days I'm staying here while you're away. Genealogical crime mysteries. Ever heard of such things?'

'Yeah, I've read some of them,' he replied. 'They're good, actually, but the characters seem to always be getting into some sort of mortal danger.'

4

'Well, look at what's happened to you in the past,' Margot said pointedly with her palms upturned.

'True,' he agreed.

'You should write a book about your exploits. Though I'm not sure anyone would believe what you get mixed up with; all in the name of genealogy,' she said.

Grace gasped, raised a finger in the air, as though struck with inspiration, and promptly left the room.

Morton turned his attention back to his PowerPoint presentation on *Researching Your Sussex Ancestors*. He had got to a point where he needed to refer to The Keep, which was the main archive repository for the county of East Sussex. He half-wondered about including a photo of his arch-nemesis, Miss Deidre Latimer, whose life's mission seemed to be annoying, embarrassing or frustrating Morton during his every visit to the archive. He had a whole collection of anecdotes about her that he could use. But he reasoned that it probably would not be very professional to use his first-ever RootsTech talk to complain about a frustrating archivist.

'Coffee? Or another bottle of wine?' Margot asked him, pointedly lifting the bottle of Diablo and finding it empty.

'Coffee, please,' he answered, trying to appear impervious to her jibes.

Grace re-entered the room, beaming. She was carrying an old vintage Imperial Model T typewriter, which she now gently set down on the table beside Morton. He couldn't help but smile at the way in which she took such great care of the lovely old machine. Despite her not quite yet being six years old, she understood well its value as a family heirloom, it having once belonged to Morton's grandmother, Anna Farrier.

He watched from his peripheral vision as she expertly wound in a sheet of quality paper, just as he had once shown her, and began to type.

The house was abruptly plunged into near silence as the drumming session ended. Instant bliss. Margot was quietly making drinks; Grace was busily typing her story, which in the wake of the drums did not seem loud at all; and Morton was able to concentrate more easily on his presentation.

He had only added a single, solitary sentence when Isaac strolled into the kitchen with his hands slung in his pockets and declared, 'I'm bored.'

Margot smiled, crouched down and said, 'Darling Isaac, only boring people get bored. And you're *not* boring. So, take yourself off and get a book or some colouring to do.'

'I hate books,' he complained.

That boy. Morton couldn't help but smile as he watched Isaac saunter out of the kitchen, the perfect example of a threenager. Then, Morton returned to his laptop to work on a brief overview of The Keep's archives. He had just opened their website to harvest some key data when Juliette opened the front door and stepped into the hallway.

'What an absolute morning,' she announced as she entered the kitchen, giving Morton and then Grace a kiss.

'Good or bad?' Margot asked as she made Morton his drink.

'I guess that all depends on the outcome,' Juliette replied, having that morning completed an examination to become a police inspector. 'A hundred and fifty questions in three hours.'

'Golly,' Margot marvelled as she placed Morton's mug of coffee down on the table in front of him.

'Multiple choice,' Juliette clarified.

'Oh, well then,' Margot countered dismissively. 'You'll get plenty right just by chance.'

'Thanks, Mum,' Juliette said, rolling her eyes at Morton. 'How are you getting on?'

'Well, I haven't really been able to concentrate much,' he replied.

'He's been far too busy curtain-twitching and drinking red wine,' Margot revealed.

'Normal day, then,' Juliette quipped.

'Are you even organised for your trip?' Margot asked him.

'Apart from finishing the presentations, yes.'

'So, you've got two presentations, yet you're going away for over a week,' Margot commented. 'What are you planning on doing the rest of the time?'

'Well, I've finally managed to get a meeting with two detectives from Reno,' he answered. 'I'm meeting them in Las Vegas to discuss reopening the case against my grandfather.'

'Good luck with *that*,' Margot scoffed, raising her eyebrows.

She wasn't wrong in her scepticism. He would need luck and plenty of it. As things stood, his maternal grandfather had been posthumously found guilty of the brutal murder of a prostitute in Reno in 1980. Morton was not necessarily seeking his grandfather's exoneration, but rather to have the case re-examined owing to the dubious outcomes of the DNA evidence analysis.

'Sounds to me as though you'll still have some spare time on your hands,' Margot said. 'Maybe you could find out what happened to Juliette's great-grandfather while you're out there. Anyway… Anyone want anything before I head back out again? The Kino's showing *Luther: The Fallen Sun* at 12:45 and I—'

'Hang on,' Morton interjected, not understanding. 'Did you say I could find out about Juliette's great-grandfather while I'm out there? Who?'

'My late husband's grandfather, Charles Hughes,' she explained.

'I literally don't have a clue what you're talking about,' Morton replied.

'Juliette's great-grandfather, Charles Hughes,' Margot repeated unhelpfully.

'What about him?'

'He lived in Las Vegas. Probably died there, too, for all we know. Upped sticks not long after the end of the First World War. Left his poor wife, Alice, and two children, Laura and

7

Arthur, behind.'

Morton angled his gaze to glare at Juliette, then turned back to face Margot. 'How's this the first time I'm ever hearing about him?'

Margot shrugged. 'I'm sure I've mentioned him before. It's you; you probably weren't listening.'

He offered a languid smile, then asked, 'Can you tell me more about him?'

'Yes, but not right now,' she replied. 'I have a date with Idris Elba. Juliette can tell you about him, though. Don't know why she hasn't. See you later.' And with that, Margot was gone out of the door.

'Tell me about your great-grandfather, then,' Morton encouraged, taking a sip of his coffee.

Juliette sighed and rested her chin in her cupped hands. 'I don't know any more than Mum just said. You're the genealogist; you tell me.'

'I doubt I'll really have time to do any research out there,' he replied. 'I've literally done one slide so far on this presentation all morning and now I've got an entire twenty-minute case study to create on top of that, when I haven't got a clue what it's going to be about.'

Juliette screwed up her face. 'Your grandfather's story would be the obvious choice.'

'Yeah, I suppose so,' he agreed. Murder, corruption, multiple abandoned foundlings all neatly wrapped up and solved with genetic genealogy. It certainly fitted the bill.

'Who else is on this DNA panel?' Juliette asked.

'I have no idea. I was going to take a look but didn't get around to it,' Morton answered, delving into his emails to find out the answer. '*Genetic Genealogy: some recent case studies. Hosted by Drew Smith, co-host of The Genealogy Guys Podcast and Genealogy Connection Podcast, various cases around the theme of family will be presented and discussed. Panellists are Jonny Perl, Diahan Southard, Roberta Estes, Morton Farrier*—' Morton stopped reading and internally gasped.

Juliette took his abrupt ending of the oration as her cue to clap and cheer, which she did in abundance. She was telling him how proud she was of him, but he had stopped listening and could only think about the final panellist, whose name he had not been able to read aloud.

Chapter Two

26th February 2023, Rye, East Sussex

It had started again. Who on earth had handed Isaac his drumsticks at this ungodly hour? Morton sat bolt upright in bed, his annoyance increasing in line with the awful racket coming from downstairs. He picked his mobile phone up from his bedside table to see the time and was slightly taken aback to see that it was just after nine in the morning. Where had his night gone? Not on sleep, that was for sure. He had stayed up long after the rest of the household had gone to bed in order to work on his RootsTech presentations. At least, that had been the idea. In reality, he'd spent most of the time before and after he'd gone to bed fretting about one of his fellow panellists on the genetic genealogy discussion panel; the one whom he'd neglected to mention to Juliette yesterday. Madison Scott-Barnhart, one of America's top and best-known investigative genetic genealogists who also happened to be his ex-girlfriend from a very long time ago.

Reading that they were to be on the same discussion panel had knocked the wind out of his sails, but he wasn't really sure why. He had spent much of the night trying to figure out what the problem was. Yes, their parting had been abrupt and had devastated him at the time, but that was in 1996 and his life had moved on completely since then. He knew that he felt nothing romantically for Maddie anymore. No lingering feelings. No what-ifs. No thoughts whatsoever of rekindling what they had once had together. Even his desire for answers and reasons as to why she had left him had faded a long time ago. Despite the chaos of family life and the ear-splitting commotion currently emanating from the lounge, he totally and utterly loved his life and felt very settled. Perhaps that was the cause of his unease?

That Juliette might be threatened by his being in Maddie's company five thousand miles away, and he was protecting her? Something had definitely prevented him from telling her that Maddie would be one of his co-panellists. Was he sparing her feelings? Staving off a potential argument? Juliette had shown twinges of jealousy when, four years ago, Maddie had first got back in touch over a cold case that her company had been hired to solve; the very case that had implicated Morton's grandfather in the 1980 murder of a prostitute. But, now that he hadn't told Juliette about Maddie, it looked as though he was indeed hiding something.

He slumped back in the bed with a noisy exhalation, firmly wishing that he had declined to speak on the genetic genealogy panel after all.

By some miracle, he had fallen back to sleep and had woken up to a now silent house. As he climbed out of bed, pulled on his dressing gown and headed downstairs, he found himself secretly hoping that Isaac might have perhaps smashed his drum kit to oblivion. He glanced into the lounge and saw that, unfortunately, the drum kit was very much still intact.

'Morning,' he greeted Margot as he entered the kitchen and made directly for the coffee machine.

'Oh, good morning,' she replied, looking up from a crossword that she was working on at the table. 'Not going for the red wine, today?'

'What? Wine? No,' he muttered. 'Far too early.'

Margot laughed. 'This time yesterday, it wasn't.'

'Fair point,' Morton agreed. 'Where is everyone?'

Margot folded the newspaper shut. 'Juliette's taken the children swimming. She said for you to use the time alone wisely.'

'Right, then,' he said, carrying his coffee to the table. He opened his laptop lid, keen to make use of this precious and rare quiet time. He found the *Researching Your Sussex Ancestors*

11

presentation open where he had left it in the early hours of this morning, with still so much left to do.

Margot stared at him and folded her arms. 'So… Charles Hughes. I'll tell you everything I know, which isn't much. But I'm sure, given your line of work, you can find out plenty more.'

'Right,' Morton said, groaning internally as he minimised the presentation and brought up a blank Word document in which to make notes.

'As I said before,' Margot continued, 'Charles Hughes was Juliette's late father's maternal grandfather, and he served in the army in the First World War…'

'Any ideas where?' Morton interrupted. 'Or in which of the services, or battalions…?'

'No idea,' Margot replied. 'Anyway, he returned home relatively unscathed to his wife, Alice, and their two children, Laura—Juliette's grandmother—and the eldest, Arthur. But by all accounts, Charles returned home a very different person. The war had changed him from a quiet, placid man into an erratic, unstable one who was prone to angry outbursts.'

'Ah… *That's* where Juliette gets it from,' Morton attempted to joke.

Margot continued, unflinching, 'Growing up for poor Laura and Arthur wasn't a pleasant experience at all. Laura very rarely spoke to me or Andrew about her childhood, but what she did say was that it was grim and that it was, frankly, a great relief the day Charles went off in search of work and never came home.'

'Did he say where he was going?' Morton asked, typing as he spoke.

Margot shook her head. 'He left a note that was all very Lawrence Oates-esque. What did he say, now? *I'm going out in search of work and I may be some time.* Accompanying the short letter was a one-pound note. And that was it. His absence went from days to weeks to months with nothing from him. Years went past and poor Alice was ostensibly left as a widow to raise

Laura and Arthur alone but with the shackles of a mirage marriage preventing her from ever moving on to a new husband.'

'I just can't believe I've never been told any of this before,' Morton commented, taking a drink of his coffee.

'Oh, you surely mustn't have been listening. It's old family lore,' she said with a thin smile.

'So, what makes you think, then, that Charles ended up in *Las Vegas* of all places?' Morton asked, considering it a highly unlikely location for Charles to find himself.

'When the Second World War came, Charles apparently remembered that he had a son who might be called up to fight, and he decided to write to him seeking forgiveness. After years in the wilderness, Charles had managed to remove himself from the devil's grip—his words, not mine—and find a path to righteousness. He said he was a regular at the Pentecostal Church, had quit smoking, drinking, gambling and prostitutes, and was now a reformed man living in Las Vegas.'

'What a catch,' Morton commented.

'Quite how he got there or why, I've no idea. You know, he even said that, after all these years of him having been absent, he would return to the marital home and simply pick up where he'd left off! Can you imagine?' Margot exclaimed. 'Poor Alice was having none of it, though. Yes, life *had* been very hard for her, living as a single woman, but the last thing she wanted was him to come waltzing back through the door again. She sent a telegram politely declining his offer.' Margot smiled. 'Arthur then, apparently, sent a not-so-polite follow-up letter that warned his father that if he ever came anywhere near the shores of England again, he'd hit him so hard he'd end up right back where he started from.'

'This is incredible,' Morton said, wondering how much of it was actually true. His job as a forensic genealogist had brought many fanciful stories his way over the years, most of which had ended up lacking evidence to back up the initial sensationalism.

'Wow. You've definitely never told me *this* before. I would have remembered.'

Margot shrugged off his comment.

Morton reviewed his typed notes. 'Any idea when it was that Charles left England?'

'No idea, sorry; just some time after the First World War ended.'

'And do you think he went directly from England to Las Vegas? Any idea what he did in the intervening years?' Morton probed, seeking something substantive with which to work.

Margot shook her head.

'Do you still have the letter that he sent?'

'I think it's in my loft somewhere. I need to pop home at some point while I'm staying here, anyway, to make sure the house is still standing and all that... I'll have a quick look to see if I can find it when I go back.'

'That would be great, thanks,' Morton said. 'If I get time when I'm out there, I'll look into it.'

'Well, we don't need any more surprises like you found with my great-grandmother, thank you very much,' Margot said, opening out the newspaper in a plain signal that the family-history lesson was over.

Morton finished his coffee, closed his laptop and rose from the table. 'Well, I suppose I'd better get up and dressed,' he said, moving towards the door with his laptop. 'Thanks for the info.'

'You're welcome,' Margot said, adding quietly, 'even though I have said it all before.'

Morton grinned, rolled his eyes and headed up to his study on the top floor of the house. He put his laptop down on his desk and turned to leave. He paused and stared at the computer for a few seconds while his brain ran over what he'd just been told about Juliette's great-grandfather. He could just take a *quick* look at some official records to see if there was any substance to the story. It should just take a few seconds to prove or disprove this strange tale. If Charles Hughes had indeed fled to

Las Vegas, there should be a raft of official documentation corroborating the story as fact.

He slid in behind his desk and reopened his laptop. The first and most obvious place to check was his own family tree on Ancestry, where he had already added a great number of Juliette's direct ancestors. Opening the tree, he typed in Charles Hughes's name. Sure enough, there he was, born in 1890, the son of Edward Hughes and Caroline Longley. Morton clicked to view his profile, which, in light of what Margot had just told him, was relatively sparse. Census images from 1891, 1901 and 1911 were saved against his name, as were original copies of his birth and marriage certificates. Curiously, no death date had been entered and Ancestry only offered one source that might have pertained to him in their entire collection, from the *UK, British Army World War I Medal Rolls Index Cards, 1914-1920* record set. If an obvious documented path to a new life in Las Vegas existed, then Ancestry was not providing it.

Morton viewed the only photograph that he had of the man, a black-and-white studio portrait of Charles, his wife and two children. Charles was dressed in a soldier's uniform, standing upright with his hand on the back of a chair upon which his wife, Alice, was sitting. In Alice's arms was a young baby and standing beside her, holding her hand, was a terrified-looking toddler. A very quick assessment of the photograph and the children's dates of birth placed the image to somewhere around early 1915, shortly after Laura Hughes's birth in January of that year.

He zoomed in to Charles's face. Despite the officiousness of his military uniform, a warmth and kindness had been captured in his bright eyes. He was clean-shaven and his short light-coloured hair was pulled over from a side-parting. As Morton stared at the picture, he had to wonder just what horrors this man would go on to witness for such an apparent seismic shift to have manifested in his personality. But this was just a photograph, a momentary snapshot, he reminded himself, not a window into the man's whole personality.

Morton closed the photograph and checked the hint for the Medal Rolls Index. Unlike the service records for the British Army, where sixty percent had been destroyed in the Second World War, the Medal Rolls Index provided information for more than ninety percent of British soldiers. The information which they contained, however, was usually minimal and rarely personal.

The reference for Charles Hughes loaded on-screen. It was a colour reproduction of a double-sided pink card with typed red headings and blue handwritten notes. The index card revealed that Charles had been a sapper with the Royal Engineers, his first theatre of war having been France and having commenced on the 18th October 1915. After the war had ended and he had returned home, Charles had been awarded the Victory Medal, the British Medal and the 1915 Star for his service.

Morton checked the references against each medal in the *UK, World War I Service Medal and Award Rolls, 1914-1920* collection but they revealed no further information about Charles or his wartime experiences. When Morton searched for Charles's actual service records, he found that they were apparently part of the burnt documents series that had unfortunately not survived. But, given the context of the story which he had just been told, Charles Hughes's life from his birth in 1890 up to the war's end in 1918 had been fairly well documented. A proof of life check beyond that point was required prior to investigating records in the US.

The next step to ascertaining Charles's presence in England was obvious: the recently released 1921 Census. Morton accessed it on the FindMyPast website and, assuming that what Margot had told him was true and that Charles had been absent from home by this point, entered the name of his wife, Alice Hughes, into the search box. *3,616 results.* He clicked *Advanced options* and added her birth year of 1892 and the name of her

daughter, Laura, in the *Other household member* box. *7 results.*
Much more workable. One entry stood out from the rest with
Alice's correct birth location of Etchingham, Sussex. Morton
clicked to view a scanned copy of the original return.

*Alice Hughes. Head. Married. Aged 28 years 6 months. Born
Etchingham, Sussex. Assistant Baker for Mr Osborne, Etchingham
Bakery.*
*Arthur Hughes. Son. Aged 9 years 1 month. Born Etchingham, Sussex.
Scholar.*
*Laura Hughes, Daughter. Aged 6 years 5 months. Born Etchingham,
Sussex. Scholar.*

Morton downloaded the entry and moved on to the next
page, which recorded the address of the property: *Brookside,
Etchingham.* Then he checked the neighbouring houses for any
sign of Charles, but there was none.

He sat back in his chair, wondering whether Margot's tale
could actually be true. Before he launched into searches across
the Atlantic, Morton wanted to be certain that Charles Hughes
had not simply been absent from the family home on that
particular night of the census. Once again, it was just a
momentary snapshot in time rather than confirmation that
Charles had indeed fled overseas.

Having spent sufficient time searching in vain for Charles in
the 1921 Census, Morton switched over to the 1939 Register.
He found Alice Hughes easily, living in Brookside, the same
house in Etchingham as she had been living in eighteen years
earlier.

*Hughes, Alice. Born 4 Dec 1892. Married. Housekeeper & Bakery
Manager.*
Hughes, Laura. Born 2 Jan 1915. Single. Unpaid domestic duties.

Yet again, no sign of Charles Hughes in the family home. The evidence was mounting. Morton started a new search in the 1939 Register for Charles but found nobody who obviously fit the bill.

There was one final proof of life check that Morton wanted to complete: a search in the death index for England and Wales.

The search produced a very long list of possible matches but an empty list of probable ones.

After more than two hours in front of his laptop, Morton had reached the tentative conclusion that Charles Hughes had indeed left his family behind and had started a new life elsewhere. Although at this stage several alternative scenarios were still possible, it was time to explore what Margot had told him had happened to Charles.

Jumping in with the US censuses, Morton decided to begin with 1950, the most recently available, and work his way backwards. He started the search with Charles's name, birth year and birth location of England. Nine hundred and seventy results were given, but when Morton looked more closely, only the top five men were actually listed as having been born in England. Morton checked each entry in turn, finding that all of them were incorrect, so he spent some time broadening, editing and refining his search criteria. But, after some more time searching, there was no obvious sign of Charles Hughes.

Moving back a decade, Morton ran the same searches in the 1940 Census but again came up empty-handed. Could Charles have died by this point? According to Margot, Charles had written to the family sometime around the outbreak of war in 1939. Maybe he'd written the letter because his own health had been failing, and he had died before the 1940 Census had been taken.

The 1930 US Census held a lot of potential promise in joining the dots between Charles's absence in England before 1921 and his writing the letter around 1939. Opening the search page, Morton entered the details, hoping to see an obvious entry close to the top of the results list. But, slowly scrolling down the first page, he was disappointed to see not a single result that jumped out at him. If Charles Hughes had given honest answers to the enumeration questions, his entry should now have been in front of Morton. If he had lied, though, then he could be any one of the 6,009 Charles Hugheses present on the census.

Undeterred, Morton edited the search down to just those men born in England. *62 Results.* He then examined every entry in turn, ruling almost all of them out completely. If the information stated was correct, then the Charles Hughes for whom he searched was not among them.

'You're *never* still in your dressing gown?' Juliette questioned, leaning on his study door. 'And it's almost five o'clock in the afternoon.'

Morton looked down at himself and nodded. 'I got a bit lost in my research.'

Juliette smiled. 'So, you're all set for your trip, then? Presentations polished and practised, I take it?'

Morton grimaced. 'Your mum really got me started on Charles Hughes and…'

Juliette groaned and turned to leave.

'I think he evaporated,' Morton called after her.

'Is that a new genealogical term that I've not yet heard of?' Juliette replied as she headed down the stairs. 'You might want to get dressed for dinner. Or not. Up to you.'

Morton stretched as he looked at the notes that he had been making on his laptop. Every single search which he had conducted had yielded a negative result, including the 1920 US Census and immigration records. Yes, he decided to coin the designation, genealogically evaporated, and bestow it upon Charles Hughes. But that very fact got under Morton's skin, and he needed to know what had happened to the man. In reality, Morton knew that he was out there somewhere and, given the number of official records that he seemed to have evaded, had been deliberately hiding.

Morton yawned, sighed and wondered where his day could have gone. Genealogically evaporated, that was where it had gone. He closed his laptop, stood up for the first time in several hours and went downstairs to join his family.

'Daddy!' Isaac greeted, clutching his plastic drumsticks in his hand.

'How's my little Animal today?' Morton asked, scooping him up for a cuddle, carrying him into the kitchen before setting him down.

'I'm not an animal,' Isaac protested with a confused, indignant frown.

Margot looked Morton up and down, and then glanced at the wall clock. 'Bit early for pyjamas and dressing gown, isn't it?'

Juliette laughed as she pulled a steaming lasagne from the oven. 'He hasn't got out of them yet.'

Morton shrugged. 'I'm acclimatising my body clock for the flight to America tomorrow. Besides,' he said, glancing over at Margot, 'it's totally your fault that I got myself stuck down a rabbit hole this afternoon.'

Isaac giggled loudly. 'Daddy went down a hole to see the rabbits!'

Morton smiled, watching as Isaac scuttled off out of the room, drumsticks ominously poised with intent in each hand. Sure enough, just as he had feared, Isaac launched into another round of dreadful drumming.

'Daddy went down a rabbit hole!' Isaac screeched, adding indeterminable extra lyrics that made him and Grace laugh.

'He's a forensic geologist, *actually*,' Morton heard Grace correct him.

'My daddy's a rabbit geologist,' Isaac chanted.

'Rabbits might be easier to research than Charles Hughes,' Morton informed Margot. 'All day I've spent working on him, instead of my Sussex ancestors' presentation, and he's nowhere to be found.'

'Sounds like you'll have to try a bit harder,' Margot suggested.

'Hmm,' he replied.

'Dinner!' Juliette shouted to nobody in particular, placing the sliced-up lasagne in the centre of the table.

'I wonder if any of his dalliances with…' Morton paused mid-sentence as Grace and Isaac entered the room, then chose his words carefully before continuing, '…his dalliances with certain ladies of the night produced any offspring who might appear in Juliette's DNA matches.'

'Well, as I said earlier,' Margot started, 'he had children by his second wife in Las Vegas, maybe they or their descendants have done one of these test things.'

'What?' Morton stammered. 'You didn't… You never mentioned that he had more children, or a *second wife*.'

'I did,' Margot insisted. 'At least…I *think* I did. I intended to, anyway.'

Morton looked at Juliette incredulously. She responded with a broad grin as she served up the lasagne.

'Remind me what you *didn't* tell me about them,' Morton asked.

'No more information than that; his letter mentioned a wife, whom he acknowledged to be illegal, and that he had had children by her.'

This new revelation changed everything. If even one of Charles Hughes's descendants with his mysterious second wife had taken a consumer DNA test, then Morton was certain that he would be able to work out Charles's assumed identity. It was a big if, but since Morton would be in Las Vegas in under twenty-four hours' time, he needed to work quickly to find out.

Chapter Three

Morton was sipping from his fourth glass of a rather good Malbec wine, made to taste all the better for its being complimentary. He was sitting in the business lounge in Terminal 5 of Heathrow Airport. The lounge was a hive of activity, with passengers coming and going prior to their flights. Huge floor-to-ceiling windows, as wide as the room itself, gave views out over one of the runways and its incessant flow of taxiing aircraft. Morton drank more wine and gazed out at a British Airways plane preparing for departure, then turned to look at the digital display board behind him. His flight was labelled simply as *On Time* and scheduled for departure in ninety minutes at 4:50 pm. Plenty of time for more wine, sandwiches and work.

On his laptop, he had Juliette's DNA matches open in different tabs; one for each of Ancestry, MyHeritage, 23andMe and Living DNA. Surely one of them held a DNA match with a descendant of Charles Hughes by his second, illegal marriage. The major problem that Morton had was that if, as he supposed, Charles Hughes had lived in the US under an alias, then his descendants would also very likely be living under that same assumed surname, perhaps totally unaware of the Hughes name hidden in their family's past.

Starting with Ancestry, Morton pulled up Juliette's DNA matches and clicked the *By parent* filter, then selected *Paternal* and *View matches*. All 7,715 of Juliette's matches on her father's side appeared in front of Morton in a long list, with the most closely related appearing at the top. Depending on when Charles had had his second family, it was possible that his children themselves might have tested. In which case, Morton would be looking for Juliette's half-great-uncle or aunt. If it were their children, he would be looking for a half-first cousin once removed.

The first step to using genetic genealogy to find someone from this branch of the family was triangulation, so Morton scrolled down the list of matches to a person known to have descended from Charles Hughes via his son, Arthur.

He settled on Clifford Hughes, whom Morton knew to be Juliette's second cousin. He clicked Clifford's name, then *Shared Matches*. He scrolled past closer, known members of Juliette's paternal family until he reached *Extended Family*, where the amount of shared DNA with these unfamiliar people instantly fell below 46 centimorgans.

Opening a new internet tab, Morton accessed The Shared cM Project tool on the DNA Painter website, where he entered 46 cM into a filter box which informed him of the most likely ways in which two people could be related sharing that quantity of DNA. Half-great-aunt or uncle and half-first cousin once removed were not statistically possible. Those numbers might well work for the generations below but would make it much harder to establish a connection.

Morton switched tabs to MyHeritage, hoping for an easier ride there. Before he started, though, he put his laptop down on the vacant seat beside him, finished the rest of his wine, then returned to the food counter and bar for another round of food and drink. Even though he was flying business class and would be more than sufficiently fed and watered throughout the flight, he filled a plate with Thai Green Curry and got another glass of Malbec, then returned to his seat.

On the MyHeritage website, Morton clicked the *DNA* tab, selected Juliette from the long list of people whose kits he managed and scrolled down the cousin-match list until he found Clifford Hughes's sister, Judy, who had tested on this site. She was stated as sharing 234 centimorgans of DNA with Juliette. Morton hit the purple *Review DNA Match* button. At the top of the page was the known information about Judy Hughes, followed by a table displaying all the possible relationships between the two women. Second cousin was estimated with a probability of 68.4%.

Morton continued down the page to *Shared DNA Matches*. In the centre of the table was a list of people who were DNA-linked to both Juliette and Judy, with the amount of centimorgans and estimated relationship stated at the side of each match. Once Morton had skipped past five known family members, he reached someone by the name of Bernadette Honeychurch. He was certain that he had never encountered anyone by that name before, let alone in Juliette's family tree. According to MyHeritage, Juliette matched Bernadette with 189 centimorgans, while Judy matched with 222. Both amounts put them squarely in the correct range for a half-first cousin once removed. Although other possibilities existed for how the three women could be related, this looked to Morton to be a promising start. Before proceeding further, he looked down the list of remaining names. *Yvette Jemmett. Edie Loveless. David Rowley*—all were DNA-matched to Juliette and Judy, but to a lesser extent than was Bernadette Honeychurch, who, so far, was the best match to investigate further.

Morton ate his curry, drank the wine and looked over at the display board to see that his flight was scheduled to leave in fifty minutes' time. He put down the glass and picked up with Bernadette Honeychurch, heartened to see the words *Appears in a family tree with 15 people that she manages* below her name and that she was *From USA*. Morton clicked *View tree* and a colourful, if slightly limited pedigree appeared on-screen. The only information pertaining to Bernadette was a birth year of 1950. Her father was listed as *<Private> Stewart* and her mother as *<Private> Lusted*. Given that information, Morton was assuming for the moment that Honeychurch was Bernadette's married name. When he clicked to see the other members of the family, he found that all surnames were prefixed by the word *<Private>*.

With so little information regarding Bernadette's parents, Morton thought it best to keep investigating Bernadette herself for the time being. Opening up Newspapers.com, he ran a search for her within the time range of 1965-1990 using the marriage filter. Fifteen results matched with his query. He slowly moved down the page, checking the listed parents' names as he went. Close to the bottom of the first page he stopped scrolling.

Mason Valley News
Yerington, Nevada
Friday, January 26, 1973

Name: Bernadette Stewart
Spouse: Donald Honeychurch
Parents: Roger and Mrs Honeychurch, Roy and Mrs Stewart

Could it be her? Morton wondered, clicking to read the full newspaper article. While he waited for it to load, he finished the last dregs of his wine. He thought about getting another glass and glanced over at the flight display board to see whether he had the time to squeeze it in. *BA275. Gate closing.*

A few short seconds passed with Morton staring at the board, frozen. The gate was closing and here he was, sitting in the lounge eating, drinking and working on an obscure branch of Juliette's family tree. He clapped his laptop lid shut, thrust it into his hand luggage, leapt up and ran for the exit.

Morton pelted down escalators, through busy shopping concourses, arriving at Gate B33 exhausted and totally out of breath. He was met by a smiling member of the British Airways staff.

'Sorry,' Morton managed to pant, handing over his passport and boarding pass. 'Too late?'

'It's quite alright, sir. You're not too late, although you are the *last* passenger to board,' the man said. 'You were about thirty seconds from a loudspeaker announcement.' He grinned, handed Morton back his documents and said, 'Have a good flight.'

'Thanks,' Morton muttered, heading briskly down the jet bridge to the waiting plane. He exhaled loudly as he stepped onto the aircraft and was greeted by a flight attendant, who seemed to Morton to check his watch and the empty jet bridge behind him before directing him to his seat.

Morton couldn't help but smile at the brand new, luxurious business class suite in which he now found himself. Placed on his window seat and waiting for him were a wash bag, pillow and duvet. He sat down, took a selfie and sent it to Juliette with the words, *Slumming it xx*, then he opened his laptop.

'Champagne or orange juice?' asked a smiling flight attendant with a tray of the proffered drinks deftly balanced on one hand.

'Champagne, please,' Morton responded.

The flight attendant handed over the drink and said, 'I'm afraid that I am going to have to ask you to put your computer away for take-off, sir.'

Morton nodded. 'Just one quick thing to check, then I'll put it away,' he promised, drinking some champagne and then placing it down on the table in front of him so that he could concentrate on reading the newspaper story that he had been about to read in the lounge. *Bernadette Stewart, Donald Honeychurch Exchange Wedding Vows Jan.10* ran the article headline. Below it was a photograph so grainy and of such poor quality that the faces of the couple in question were almost impossible to see. But it was the text under the photo that Morton was really interested in.

Miss Bernadette Stewart became the bride of Mr. Donald Honeychurch on January 10 in the First Christian Church of Las Vegas. Miss Lena

Stewart, the bride's sister, was the maid of honour and Mr. Traux, the best man. The new Mrs. Honeychurch is the daughter of Mr. and Mrs. Roy Stewart Jr. of Ely, White Pine. She is a graduate of White Pine schools and was a receptionist for Messrs. Trunk & Glazier solicitors. Mr. Honeychurch is the son of Mr. and Mrs. James Honeychurch of Fernley, Lyon County. He is a graduate of Fernley schools and is manager of the Union 76 station. The couple is at home in the Lahontan Motel Trailer Park in Fernley.

Morton reread the story, finding that the information it contained tied with that which he already knew. The most intriguing aspect was Roy Stewart's name. Did the fact that it had the suffix of *junior* mean that Morton had discovered the name that Charles Hughes had adopted when he flitted off to America? It wasn't conclusive, but it was certainly the next avenue that he would be exploring. For now, though, it was time to sit back and enjoy the flight. He closed his laptop, placed it into his personal locker beside his seat and pulled forward the video screen to see what inflight entertainment was on offer.

As he scrolled through page after page of available movies, his mobile sounded with an incoming message. It was a selfie of Juliette in their lounge at home. Behind her, Isaac was sitting at his drum kit with his sticks in the air, mid-strike, and a manic look on his face, and, to his side, Grace was standing with her hands covering her ears. *Wish you were here?!? xx*

Morton smiled, settled back in his chair and sipped his champagne. Although he missed his family already, he was going to enjoy his first solo adventure across the pond.

Chapter Four

28th February 2023, Las Vegas, Clark County, Nevada, USA

Morton woke in a total daze, moving to sit bolt upright and staring at the strange, flickering lights in the corner of the room. When he just could not make sense of what they might be, he leant over to wake Juliette, but found that she wasn't there. Her side of the bed was cold and empty. Was she working nights? He swung his legs out of the bed and felt an unfamiliar carpet texture beneath his feet as he slowly walked towards the lights. He quickly realised that they were coming from behind the curtains, so he slowly opened them to find that he was staring at the Eiffel Tower. A grounded hot air balloon with the word *Paris* in large flashing letters beside the tower confirmed that he had absolutely lost his mind. How had he ended up in France?

It took a good few seconds of thought and scrutinising the neon lights in the distance beyond the Eiffel Tower for him to finally understand that he was not in Paris at all, and Juliette wasn't on a night shift. He was in fact alone, staying in the Planet Hollywood Hotel on the famous Las Vegas Strip.

He sighed, slightly relieved and slightly perturbed at how long his hopelessly addled brain had taken to orientate himself. He was more exhausted than he could remember ever having been before. He had already been tired, emotional and with a splitting headache when the plane had touched down at the Harry Reid International Airport yesterday. He'd eaten too much, drunk too much and had spent the entirety of the flight watching films instead of getting some sleep or working on his RootsTech presentations. The last film that he had finished watching, just minutes before landing, *Downton Abbey: A New Era*, had left him sobbing over his Gin Zing to the point that he had been asked by the flight attendant if there had been anything that he could do to assist. Then there had been the absurdly long queues at the Customs and Border Protection, delays at baggage claim and a lengthy line to get an Uber to the hotel. He had collapsed into bed at just after ten o'clock at night local time, which, if his currently challenged brain had calculated it correctly, would have been somewhere around 6 am in the UK.

Morton headed back to bed with a long groan. He was finally here, his first time in this infamous city, but totally lacking the energy needed to explore it. Tomorrow, after meeting with the detectives handling his grandfather's case, he would be flying the short hop on to Salt Lake City for RootsTech. His heart pounded at the realisation that he was going to be delivering his unfinished talk on *Researching Your Sussex Ancestors* in just two days' time and delivering a twenty-minute presentation the following day on a subject about which he had yet to write a single word.

He sighed at the thought of seeing Maddie again. Then an idea came to his mind: *she* must have been made aware by now of who her fellow panellists were going to be. Perhaps she herself might have withdrawn to avoid any potential awkwardness. He couldn't imagine for a second that she would want to be on a panel with him any more than he did with her. He took his mobile phone from the bedside table and opened the RootsTech 2023 conference app. From the main menu, he clicked *Speakers* and scrolled down to *Barnhart, Madison Scott* and touched her name, which in turn led him to her profile. At the top of the page was a headshot and Morton looked at her face for the first time in many years. She hadn't really changed much, although it appeared that the nose stud and heavy eyeliner were now a thing of the past. Her curly blonde hair, worn to her shoulders, was exactly the same, though.

He gazed at her picture, memories of their time together randomly spooling into his tired mind. He remembered their collaborative research work, visits to museums and meals out together. Then, with stark clarity, came the recollection of the day when he had just returned to their shared flat only to find her gone. Just a short note to say that she was returning to America, without even the briefest explanation as to why. She had left him no contact details and he had known too little about her previous life to attempt to track her down. In the years since her departure, he'd come to view her as a mini whirlwind that had entered his life with her characteristic melodrama and then had exited it in much the same fashion. He pondered whether she might still be the same.

Moving past Maddie's profile picture, he read her short biography.

Madison Scott-Barnhart AG ® is a professional genealogist, instructor and one of the foremost investigative genetic genealogists in the field. She is the CEO and founder of Venator, a Salt Lake City-based company that specializes in working with Law Enforcement on suspect cases and unidentified human remains. Notable recent cases that Maddie and her team have solved using investigative genetic genealogy are The Winterset Butcher, The Broadview Strangler, The Chester Creek Murders *and the company's first live case,* The Sawtooth Slayer.

It was quite a CV and one which left Morton feeling intimidated and wondering what on earth he thought he was doing, trying to co-present alongside such huge names in the field.

He took a breath and scrolled down to *Sessions.* Maddie was delivering three talks, one of which was *Genetic Genealogy: some recent case studies.* He was still listed as a panellist, alongside Diahan Southard, Roberta Estes, Jonny Perl and Madison Scott-Barnhart. Brilliant. There was no going back now. There was also no question; he had to use his grandfather's story as his case study—with its connection to Rosie Hart and the foundlings that she had left in shop doorways around England—if it were to come anywhere near holding its own against that which his ex-girlfriend would likely be discussing. Then he noticed a sentence which made his blood run cold: *This talk will be live-streamed.*

Live-streamed? Morton gulped, as the horror of his situation sank in.

He quickly closed the RootsTech conference app in case he made any further unpleasant discoveries and came to the realisation that he wasn't going to get back to sleep any time soon. What was the time, anyway? Goodness knows what time it was in England, but it was five fifty-five in the morning in Las Vegas. He really only had today to explore the city, so he needed to shut the talks and the huge doubts out of his mind, shower and get out of the hotel.

Morton stepped out of the elevator into the hotel lobby. If he hadn't seen the crisp bright blue sky from his bedroom window just moments before, he would never have believed that it was even daylight outside, given the subdued interior of the hotel with not a speck of natural daylight anywhere. The reception desk, backlit in neon pink, looked exactly as it had upon his arrival late last night and the large open space was equally as busy now as it had been then, with people coming and going to the casino. Morton's past forays into gambling amounted to little more than spending a few pounds in two-pence pieces on the coin-pusher machines in the Stade amusement arcades on Hastings seafront as a young boy. He had some premium bonds and played the lottery very occasionally, but taking financial risks was not his thing. Still, gambling was the city's big draw, and it was something that he should at least take a quick look at since he had come all this way.

The casino itself was only marginally brighter than the hotel lobby, lit by garish, purple and pink neon strips that divided the room from the upper floors. The smell of the place baffled Morton's senses. It was a smoky, slightly noxious, stale, fruity, muddled air freshener that wafted over him as he walked past row upon row of slot machines and one-armed bandits. Despite the early hour of the morning, many of the machines were already occupied and some keen gamblers were managing to play out of a tub full of coins, across several machines at the same time, a beer bottle in one hand and a cigarette in the other.

The slot machines gave way to a long bank of blackjack, poker and roulette tables, with eager croupiers demonstrating their shuffling prowess or moving stacks of colourful chips around the table in a way which was unfathomable to Morton.

He paused beside an active game of roulette, watching the ball circle the wheel on the table. His eye was drawn to black twenty-two and he mentally committed a hundred dollars to his gut feeling. He watched as the ball danced its final jig before settling on the wheel. Red fourteen. He definitely shouldn't gamble for real, he thought, heading on past a busy bar and on to another long section of slot machines.

He continued walking, until he realised that he was entirely lost in a gambler's paradise. He turned three hundred and sixty degrees, and his entire field of view was the same neon-lit machines and tables in every direction. As he unsuccessfully tried to backtrack in the direction from which he had just come, he couldn't help but smile at the horrific idea of becoming trapped in here for hours, endlessly searching for an elusive exit, with no idea of whether it be night or day.

In the end, Morton gave up trying to escape and asked a poker croupier for directions.

'Which exit?' the croupier replied, as though the conundrum were purely one of choice rather than the mere ability to find any at all. He kept his luring eyes on Morton while dramatically pulling apart his deck of cards as though it were an accordion.

Morton shrugged. 'I don't... I don't honestly care. I just want to get outside. Alright, how about the main Strip?'

The croupier smiled, threw the cards into his left hand and pointed with his right. 'Keep heading towards that giant glitterball over there. Once you get there, hang a right at the poker tables and keep going straight until you hit the Britney Spears slots. Behind those, you're gonna see a red path that leads to the Gordon Ramsay Burger joint. Then past a whole bunch of shops and then right out onto the glorious Las Vegas Boulevard, yes siree.' His sentence crescendoed to an alarmingly loud finale.

'Thanks,' Morton said, having only selectively retained in his mind a giant glitterball, Britney Spears and Gordon Ramsay.

'You want a game before you leave?' the croupier asked with a smile, flicking through the whole deck of cards in one hand, purposely right in front of Morton's face.

Morton tapped his pockets. 'I'm all out of money,' he said, too embarrassed to admit the truth that he didn't have the first clue how to play poker.

'Welcome to Vegas,' the croupier chuckled.

'Thanks,' Morton said, heading off towards the giant glitterball as directly as the myriad of slot machines would allow.

Much to his surprise, he was able to recall the croupier's instructions and finally achieved his escape from the gambling labyrinth.

Outside, the air was warm, and the sky was the most perfect shade of blue. He breathed in deeply as he took in his surroundings. Right in front of him was the Eiffel Tower that had so startled him a few hours ago and across the street one block away was the famous Caesar's Palace. Without paying much thought to his destination, Morton headed down the palm-tree-lined street, using the escalator-fed footbridges that allowed people to cross over the eight lanes of noxious vehicle traffic. He passed the Flamingo Hotel and an assortment of famous bars, restaurants and casinos as he continued aimlessly down Las Vegas Boulevard.

Passing signs advertising such diverse activities as *Zombie Burlesque, Sci-Fi Wedding Chapel, Twilight Zone Monster Mini Golf* and the *Museum of Selfies*, Morton wandered off the main drag and crossed down the less glitzy Sammy Davis Junior Drive and past a mini encampment of homeless people on the side of the pavement. As he walked, he wondered what the place might have been like in Charles Hughes's day; or Roy Stewart's, if that was indeed the name that he had adopted. So far, he had seen nothing at all that dated back as far as the 1920s.

After several minutes more walking, Morton found himself in a similar situation to the one that he had faced first thing this morning, when he opened the curtains and thought himself in Paris. He was standing at the junction of Tropicana and Las Vegas Boulevard. Behind him was a huge, gold lion statue, the icon of the MGM empire. Directly across the street was the fairytale-castle-style Excalibur Hotel, replete with multiple red and blue minarets, whilst, on the opposite side of the road, there were a series of buildings replicating New York City, including the Statue of Liberty.

To round off this picture of total lunacy, a man wearing a pink dressing gown cycled right past him with an Alsatian dog wearing sunglasses in a basket on the back of his bike.

He was drawn back to reality by a long groan originating in his stomach. His body clock was all over the place and, right now, it wanted food and some rest. He slowly headed back in the direction of Planet Hollywood, looking for somewhere to eat as he went. As he walked, he saw the huge red logo of the *Bubba Gump Shrimp Company* on the third floor of a building in the same complex as his hotel. Perfect, he thought, riding the escalators up and entering the fishing-wharf-themed restaurant. He was seated at a window table with red leather chairs, surrounded by old car number plates fixed to the walls. The view from the window gave out over the eight lanes of congested traffic to the Bellagio Hotel and Caesar's Palace behind that. Morton's focus drifted back into the room. The wooden table in front of him was etched with phrases from the *Forrest Gump* movie. The one directly facing him made him smile: *Stupid is as stupid does.*

Was he stupid not to have withdrawn from the genetic genealogy panel, when he knew that Maddie would be there? Probably. He was more stupid, though, to have not told Juliette that Maddie would be a co-panellist. Should he tell her this omitted detail now, casually, via text message? What about the fact that it was going to be live-streamed? Tell her that, too? If he were to tell her, then she would be sure to watch it live, which only added to the pressure that he was feeling; but if he went on keeping it from her, then she would question him as to why. God, but it was a nightmare.

'Good morning, sir,' a young waitress with bright blue lipstick and matching eye shadow greeted him. 'My name's Melody-Jane and I will be your server. What can I get for ya, today?'

'Oh, so sorry,' he apologised. 'I haven't chosen yet.'

'Not a problem at all. I'll be back in just a few minutes. Take your time, now.'

Morton thanked her and tried hard to focus on the menu, but tiredness was enticing him towards his bed and giving him the idea of just skipping food altogether. If he was going to adjust to the time zone here, he needed to fight the drowsiness, and so, his first choice from the menu was a large coffee. His second choice was the *Shrimper's Heaven*, which consisted of fried shrimp, coconut shrimp, tempura shrimp, fries, cocktail sauce, Cajun marmalade and tempura sauce.

When Melody-Jane next returned, he was ready for her and placed the order.

'Great,' she commented, noting it on her pad. 'Where are you visiting from? Isn't that a British accent?'

'Yes, it is,' he replied. 'I'm from a small English coastal town in the south. Basically, it's a complete opposite kind of a place to Vegas.'

Melody-Jane chuckled. 'And what brings you to Sin City?' She asked, looking at his wedding ring, before adding, 'Or is it a 'What happens in Vegas, stays in Vegas' kinda situation?'

'No. Nothing's *happening* in Vegas,' he said, probably a little too defensively. 'I'm sort of passing through on my way to Salt Lake City... But I *am* interested in any buildings left standing here from the 1920s-era?'

Melody-Jane's face fell. 'In Vegas, if something's old, we just tear it right on down and build something bigger and better in its place.' She shrugged. 'Well, or we blow it up. Either way, old is *out* in Vegas: *Not* cool. I'll be right back with that coffee for ya.'

'Right,' Morton said, the historian inside him softly sobbing. He pulled out his mobile phone and ran a Google search for *historic Las Vegas*. Melody-Jane had been right, there really wasn't much left. There was an old Mormon Fort Downtown that had been the first structure built by people of European descent in what would become the city of Las Vegas. Impressive, Morton thought, for a city supposedly hell-bent on continually erasing its very own history. If he had time, he would visit the fort, but it wasn't quite what he was looking for.

Returning to his search, he found several references to Block 16 as being the original city settlement, which appeared to have been an area on North First Street, between Ogden and Stewart Avenues. According to various websites, this district was the only one in Las Vegas townsite where, from 1905 on, liquor had been able to be sold. This notorious area had eventually adapted to include gambling, prostitution and quick divorce.

Morton looked the site up on Google Maps, wondering, as he did so, if Charles Hughes might have come to this particular area of the city and, if so, if his new chosen surname of Stewart had any connection to Stewart Avenue. He found that the remnants of Block 16 were north of his current location in Downtown Las Vegas. There would be no time for him to visit there this side of RootsTech.

'Here you go,' Melody-Jane practically sang as she set a huge vat of coffee down in front of him. 'Your food'll be right out.'

'Thank you very much,' he said. 'Do you happen to have a pen that I could borrow, please?'

'Why, sure,' Melody-Jane replied, handing him a biro from her top pocket.

'Thanks,' Morton said.

'You're so welcome, honey.'

Morton sipped the coffee, willing the caffeine to pass quickly into his veins to help keep his eyes open, then opened out a serviette in front of him. Crudely and quickly, he drew out the family tree that linked Juliette to her second cousins, Clifford and Judy, with Charles Hughes at the top. He then added a dotted vertical line down from Charles and wrote *Roy Stewart Jnr?* Then another dotted vertical line from him down to Bernadette Stewart.

To verify Bernadette Stewart's lineage, Morton opened up the FamilySearch website and used the Research Wiki to find records for White Pine County, Nevada, where, according to her marriage report, Bernadette had grown up. The records that he needed appeared to be held on the FamilySearch website itself. However, from his research into his grandfather's ill-fated trip to Reno, Nevada, Morton knew that certain counties' records were not included.

He entered Bernadette's details and smiled. White Pine County births for this period had been transcribed with an accompanying scan of the original record. He clicked on her name and her birth certificate appeared on his phone screen.

Place of Birth: White Pine, East Ely, Nevada
Name of hospital or institution: Steptoe Valley Hospital
Usual residence of Mother: 110 11th St, East Ely, White Pine, Nevada

Full name of child: Bernadette Stewart
Date of birth: June 6, 1950

Sex: Female

Father of child: Roy Stewart Jr
Color or race: White
Age at the time of this birth: 21 years
Birthplace: Prescott, Arizona
Usual occupation: Salesman

Mother of child: Addie Lusted
Color or race: White
Age at the time of this birth: 19 years
Birthplace: Gold Creek, Nevada
Usual occupation: housewife

The document went on to record additional details about the birth, but none which would assist Morton further with his current enquiry.

He scribbled the basic details onto the serviette, taking particular interest in the fact that Roy Stewart Jr had been born in 1929 in Prescott, Arizona. So far, there was no link to Las Vegas. Although, when Morton looked Prescott up on Google Maps, he found that it was only 250 miles away. So, perhaps in the apocryphal story of Charles Hughes's absconding, the latter location had morphed into the more glamorous-sounding and renowned Las Vegas.

One thing that the document certainly did prove was that this person referred to here was the same Bernadette Stewart who DNA-matched with Juliette. What next? Morton pondered, drinking several mouthfuls of his coffee but having yet to feel any more awake.

Both the 1930 US Census and Roy Stewart Jr's birth certificate—*if* it existed online—could turn out to be equally illuminating. Wanting to gather as many solid facts as he could, Morton opted to search for the birth record in Prescott,

Yavapai County.

The FamilySearch Research Wiki directed him to *Arizona Birth Certificates 1887-1935* on MyHeritage. Morton entered Roy Stewart's name, year and place of birth, leaving the other fields blank.

He smiled at the top result, where *Roy Stewart Sr* was listed as the father. He clicked *View record* and a scanned original appeared.

Place of birth: 209 S. Pleasant, Prescott, Yavapai County, Arizona
Full name of child: Roy Stewart Jr
Sex: Male
Legitimate: Yes
Date of birth: September 12, 1929

Father full name: Roy Stewart Sr
Residence: Prescott, Arizona
Color or race: White
Age at last birthday: 39
Birthplace: England
Trade: Laborer

Mother full name: Beulah Hennes
Residence: Prescott, Arizona
Color or race: White
Age at last birthday: 29
Birthplace: Kansas
Trade: Housewife
Number of children born of this mother: 1

The age and birth location fitted Charles Hughes exactly and the DNA pointed to one of Bernadette's direct and close ancestors; but was this enough proof? It wasn't. At least not for

Morton. He noted the details on another serviette, then went in search of Roy Stewart's marriage to Beulah Hennes. FamilySearch suggested a range of possible options for where to conduct this search, with overlapping records at Ancestry, FindMyPast and FamilySearch.

Morton feared another change of name was looming as he worked through each record set in turn, finding nothing that matched at the first two companies. As he entered the details into FamilySearch, Melody-Jane re-appeared, this time with his food.

'Here we go with Shrimper's Heaven!' she said, gleefully placing down a huge silver platter of shrimp sitting on a sheet of mocked-up newspaper.

'Wowsers,' Morton commented at the quantity of food. 'Good job I've got an appetite.'

Melody-Jane giggled. 'I'll be right back with a refill for your coffee,' she said, turning on her heel and walking away before he could decide on the wisdom of having another gigantic vat of caffeine.

Morton attacked the food ravenously, as though he had not eaten for several weeks. Melody-Jane returned with a steaming coffee pot and filled his mug nearly back up to the brim. 'How's the food?' she asked.

'Really delicious,' he answered.

'Great. Enjoy your meal.'

As Morton stuffed a tempura shrimp into his mouth, he picked up his mobile phone and entered Roy Stewart's marriage to Beulah Hennes into the FamilySearch *Arizona, County Marriages, 1871-1964* record set. The top two results out of forty-four—appearing to be identical—looked correct. Morton clicked the top entry and a scanned copy of an original marriage license and marriage certificate opened on-screen. The license provided little information, serving only as the permission required in order to marry. The marriage certificate itself was more revealing.

This certifies that on the 15ᵗʰ January 1929, Roy Stewart and Beulah Hennes were united in marriage at Phoenix, Arizona according to the laws of Arizona and by the authority of the foregoing License, by Rev. H.L. Faulkner in the presence of Mrs Herman Bates and Mrs Otis Kent, who have attached their signatures as witnesses to said marriage ceremony.

At the bottom of the page were the witnesses' signatures, along with those of the officiating minister, and the bride and groom.

Morton couldn't help but feel disappointed. There were no parent names or further details to confirm that Roy Stewart was indeed Charles Hughes and the whole certificate had been transcribed by a clerk, so none of the signatures were by their own hands.

Eating another shrimp, Morton clicked back to the two identical marriage results, then hit the second one to see if it was indeed a duplicate. It wasn't identical at all; it was the affidavit for the marriage license. Given what he now knew about Charles Hughes, Morton couldn't help but smile at the wording that Roy Stewart had attested to be true.

Roy Stewart, being first duly sworn upon his oath does declare, depose and certify: That Roy Stewart is his true name; that his age is 39 years; that he is a resident of Prescott, Yavapai; that he is of the Caucasian race; that he is not related to Beulah Hennes and that he has not been granted a divorce by any Court in the State of Arizona within the past year.

Much to Morton's delight, at the bottom of the statement was Roy Stewart's original signature.

He drank more coffee, yet felt more tired than ever as he opened up another internet page on his mobile phone and navigated to the original copy of Charles and Alice's 1911 marriage certificate on his family tree.

When the image loaded, Morton hurriedly zoomed in to Charles Hughes's signature.

Although the two names were entirely different, there was little doubt in Morton's mind that they had been written by the same person. The size and slant of the letters were the same, but the giveaway was the letter *a*—appearing almost to have been written backwards—clearly repeated across both names.

The evidence that Morton had gathered thus far was sufficiently compelling for him to accept that Charles Hughes and Roy Stewart were one and the same man.

He took in a long breath, pleased to have reached this conclusion, but was so absolutely dog-tired as not to be able to think much more on anything today. He started to eat another shrimp, yawned and then placed the food back down on his plate. He was done—and in so many ways.

He gazed out of the window, noticing for the first time that the famous water fountains outside the Bellagio Hotel had started their dramatic and colourful display. He watched, mesmerised by the dancing water.

'Sir, are you okay?'

Morton's eyes pinged open, his heart racing. He looked up at Melody-Jane and knew from the relief on her face that he must have nodded off for a few seconds and she had worried that there had been something wrong with him. 'No. Yes, I'm fine, thank you. Just drifted off, there, for a moment—jet lag.'

Melody-Jane smiled. 'You were slumped down in your seat, there, for quite a long while…' she said, letting the accusation hang in the air.

Morton grimaced. 'Really? How long?' he asked, not wanting to hear the answer.

'Maybe forty-five minutes,' she answered. 'Or a little more.'

'Sorry,' he mumbled. 'I think it's high time I went to bed.'

'You know, I think so, too.'

Chapter Five

1st March 2023, Las Vegas, Clark County, Nevada, USA

Morton was sitting alone at a table for four in Vesta Coffee Roasters. Judging by the bright young things seated at laptops along the length of the window-side bar, this was the place to be for out-of-office working. The coffee shop had an urban industrial feel with concrete floors, painted white brick walls and exposed ceiling ducting that all felt slightly incongruous with the glitzy façade that Morton had encountered in the rest of the city. Best of all, though, there wasn't a single slot machine in sight.

Finishing the final mouthful of salmon toast breakfast, Morton slid the plate to one side and sipped his latte. With a nutritious breakfast and decent coffee inside him, plus a much-needed eleven hours of uninterrupted sleep, he now felt vaguely human once again. And, to cap it all, he had just created the final slide of his *Researching Your Sussex Ancestors* presentation.

He looked at his watch. The two Reno detectives were due here in forty-five minutes. Valuable time in which he could begin working on his genetic genealogy presentation. Instead, however, he opened up the expanding family tree for Charles Hughes, whose entry now bore the additional fact of *Also Known As Roy Stewart*. Morton had managed to achieve nothing more on the case following his suffering the indignity of falling asleep at the restaurant table yesterday.

Now, with some concrete facts tying Charles, aka Roy, to the Arizona and Nevada area in the late 1920s, Morton wanted to fill in the gaps on his timeline. First, though, he typed out a message to Bernadette Honeychurch that mentioned the MyHeritage DNA match and that it appeared to be through her grandfather, Roy Stewart, via a previous relationship in England. For the time being, he glossed over the minor issues of desertion, bigamy and deception, hoping first to hear back from her. He sent the same message to Yvette Jemmett, Edie Loveless and David Rowley, all of whom were linked to Juliette in the same way.

Knowing that Roy and Beulah were living in Prescott, Yavapai County, Arizona, at the time of their son's birth in the autumn of 1929, Morton opened up the search page for the 1930 US Census and entered Roy's and Beulah's names, along with the location.

The top result looked to be correct, in spite of the fact that their surname had been recorded under the spelling of *Stuart*. Morton clicked to view the original return, finding that the family had been living in a rented house on North Pleasant Street in the city of Prescott.

He slowly scanned his eyes along the entry. Apart from his name and his age at first marriage, the rest of the information about Roy Stewart matched with that of Charles Hughes.

Having saved the entry to Charles's profile, Morton ran a search for him ten years later. The 1940 Census showed Roy and Beulah continuing to live in Prescott, only this time with a vastly increased family. There were now six children to the couple, ranging in ages from five months through to Roy Junior who had been recorded as eleven years old. Morton guessed that Yvette Jemmett, Edie Loveless and David Rowley descended from these additional children.

Ten years later, in the final census available to offer a snapshot into Charles Hughes's second family, Roy was recorded with Beulah and their six children living in Prescott, where he was working as a plumber.

The search algorithms at Ancestry had now accepted Charles's dual life and began to offer further records pertaining to his second incarnation. The one of most interest to Morton was the link to a burial on FindAGrave.

He clicked through to the website, finding an image of a low, granite headstone on which was inscribed: *Roy Stewart 1890-1971. Husband and Father. His walk said it all.*

The inscription felt illuminating, somehow saying a great deal between the lines. There was no *In loving memory* or *Much loved husband* or *Adoring father*; just a bizarre reference to his walk. Was that all that his second wife and six kids had found to say about him? *His walk said it all.* An arrogant swagger came to Morton's mind. How else could he have walked, given the life that he had apparently led?

The man had died in July 1971, and lay buried in Miracle Valley Cemetery, which seemed somehow poetic to Morton. A miracle that he had gone to the grave evading the law and mortal judgement.

Morton saved the document to Charles Hughes's burgeoning profile, then wondered if his death certificate might be available online. Once again, he used the FamilySearch Research Wiki to ascertain where such records might be. Knowing that only limited records were freely available online for the neighbouring state of Nevada, Morton wasn't overly hopeful, despite the fact that the first suggested link was for *1800-1972, Arizona Genealogy Record Search* at the Arizona Department of Health Services.

He filled in the search form with Roy Stewart's name and year of death and hit enter. *Two results*, the second of which matched with the month and year recorded on the headstone. Morton clicked the name and a PDF death certificate opened up. It was him.

He carefully read the document, learning that Roy Stewart had died from a cerebral haemorrhage at his home in Miracle Valley, Cochise County, Arizona, where he had been living for eight years. His widow, Beulah, was marked down as the informant and, interestingly, she had stated *Unknown* to the names of Roy's mother and father. Had he kept his entire past life hidden from Beulah? Morton wondered, or had he offered a blended background of fantasy and reality, as seen in the reference to his birthplace in England?

Once he had saved the death certificate to Charles Hughes's profile, Morton scrutinised what he had discovered about the man. In England, he had his 1890 birth certificate, entries for the 1891, 1901 and 1911 censuses, his marriage certificate to Alice and confirmation that he had served in and survived the First World War. In America, Morton had found him on the 1930, 1940 and 1950 censuses, located his death certificate, burial location and his 1929 marriage certificate to Beulah.

But what about the gap between 1918 and 1929? Where had he been during that period? He wasn't showing up in England in any obvious way on the 1921 census, so Morton was working on the presumption that he was already in America by that point. He opened up the 1920 US Census and ran a search for Roy Stewart, born 1890 in England. The top results looked incorrect, so Morton continued down the page, clicking on various possible entries as he went, but—unless the man had been lying, which was entirely possible—nothing matched up with the documentation on either side of this apparent chasm in his life.

Morton edited the search from Roy Stewart to Charles Hughes, not knowing at what point the name change might have occurred. Once again, the search appeared fruitless.

As two men—who had the bulky build and no-nonsense demeanour of stereotypical detectives—entered the coffeeshop, Morton wondered if it even mattered that an eleven-year gap existed during the now very well-documented life of an eighty-one-year-old man?

The two men clocked Morton as he smiled and awkwardly stood to greet them, before doubting himself and pausing midway through rising until they reciprocated his smile.

'Mormon Farrier?' one of the men asked officiously, moving towards him.

That was a new one. He'd been called Norton and Mortimer

in his time, but never Mormon. 'Hello, there. It's Morton, actually,' he corrected.

'Oh, sorry,' he apologised. 'Slip of the tongue. I guess it's because you said you were heading up to Salt Lake.'

His friend, tall with cropped blond hair, laughed.

The first man shrugged and looked at the two empty chairs opposite Morton. He was in his early thirties, had a thick neck, shaved head and steely grey eyes that restlessly scanned the room. 'Mind if we swap seats? I really don't like to sit with my back to the room,' he said. 'Even off-duty.'

'Sure. Yes. Not a problem,' Morton said, standing up and switching sides.

'Thanks,' the detective said, assuming Morton's seat and only then offering his solid hand to shake. 'I'm Detective Mark Marriott. And this—,' he introduced, '—is my partner in crime, Detective Duane Reckowski.'

'Hi, there,' Duane said, shaking Morton's hand. He was the younger of the two and, judging by their interactions so far, the less senior of the pair. It was going to be the more vocal of the two detectives that Morton would need to convince.

'Thank you so much for agreeing to meet me,' Morton began. 'I've been trying to get this case re-examined for quite a while.'

Another shrug from the detective. 'I've taken over the cold case unit and I'm happy to take a look at it for you. But what you've got to understand is that our resources are tight. I'm sitting on thirty-two unsolved homicides that are all clawing for my tiny budget and here you've got a case that was closed that you want me to *re*open.'

Duane chuckled and glanced down at the table, as though he were having his time wasted.

'So,' Mark continued with a thin, challenging smile. 'You've got the time that it takes me to drink my coffee to convince me to take another look. Then our vacation starts and we're hitting the casinos.'

Morton nodded. He understood fully that what he was asking was a stretch. He stood up. 'What type of coffee do you guys want?'

'Just regular coffee for me with a splash of half and half,' Mark replied.

'Just black for me,' Duane said.

Morton went up to the counter and bought the drinks, noticing as he waited that the two detectives were conversing quietly together and, given how they kept looking in his direction, he guessed that it was about him. He had his work cut out but, unlike his readiness for RootsTech, he had come fully prepared for this meeting.

He carried the coffees over to the table, set them down and retook his new place at the table before picking up the manilla folder that he had created for the case. 'So...' Morton began, opening the file to the first page which summarised the murder of Reno prostitute, Candee-Lee Gaddy. 'As you know, her body was found in Governors Bowl Park in December 1980 with multiple stab wounds. A DNA sample was matched to my grandfather, Alfred Farrier, through investigative genetic genealogy. However, blood detected on the murder weapon matched neither Candee-Lee Gaddy nor my grandfather. The blood was found just at the base of the blade at the top of the handle, that would very likely have come from the person holding it, which I think casts more than reasonable doubt on his having been the murderer.' Morton paused for an anticipated dramatic effect that he'd seen time and again in the movies.

'SODDI,' Duane muttered, picking up his drink.

'Pardon me?' Morton replied.

'Some Other Dude Did It,' Mark explained. 'It's a common defence strategy.'

Morton sat back, feeling rebuffed. 'But there was someone else's blood on the knife. Someone who'd been holding it and whose hand must have caught on the blade. And, what's more, it isn't just *some other dude* that I'm accusing, it's an exact person,' he said, turning the page and holding up a black-and-white photo. 'This person, Rosie Hart. She was a prostitute from a criminal family in England.'

Mark rubbed his stubbly chin. 'She doesn't exactly sound like your textbook Reno prostitute murderer.'

'Exactly,' Morton countered. 'That's what she hoped would happen. The truth is, I believe her to have been responsible for several murders in England, some of which are actively being examined by police over there.'

'Motive?' Duane asked.

'All of them—including my grandfather—were men that she sought revenge on for leaving her pregnant.'

Duane sighed and drank a big mouthful of coffee, which made Morton panic that his time was really about to run out.

'Rosie Hart was in Reno the day that Candee-Lee Gaddy was murdered,' Morton quickly added.

'Can you prove that?' Mark asked.

'I can. She got run over by a bus there and died.'

'That's shitty luck,' Duane commented with a dry laugh.

'Are you saying that the genetic genealogy DNA analysis on the sample that implicated your grandfather was *wrong*?' Mark pushed.

Morton shook his head. 'No, not at all. I'm sure my grandfather had a…well…a liaison with Candy-Lee but I don't think he killed her.'

'SODDI,' Duane repeated, much to Morton's annoyance.

'But what if some other dude *did* do it?' Morton retorted. 'Could you not at least do IGG on the second sample like you did the first?'

Mark's eyes widened and he glanced sideways to Duane. He drew in a long breath and said, 'Listen. As I said, I've got thirty-two unsolved homicides that I can't afford to put through this genetic genealogy process.' He shrugged. 'How do I justify *that* to those victims' families?'

'Or the chief, for that matter,' Duane cut in.

'Or the chief,' Mark agreed.

'What about if Venator—the company who did the IGG on the case—did their part for free?' Morton blurted out.

Mark finished his drink, then said, 'If you can get all of the testing and analysis done at no cost to my department, then it'll make a big difference. But don't forget—just getting a DNA match doesn't solve the case; it's just another tool. I've got to build a case against this Rosie person.'

'I understand,' Morton said, handing over the dossier that he had compiled. 'Everything you need's in there.'

'I'll take a look,' Mark promised, taking the proffered file.

Duane slid his chair backwards and stood. 'If this Rosie woman is dead and your grandfather is also dead, why do you care so much about who gets the blame forty years on?'

'I believe the wrong person was convicted and that needs redressing,' Morton answered simply.

'Welcome to America,' Mark said, thrusting his hand forwards.

Morton shook his hand, unsure if his comment related to the injustice in the Candee-Lee Gaddy murder case or was a genuine welcome to his country. 'Thank you very much for your time and meeting with me, here.'

'You're welcome. Enjoy your trip to Salt Lake, Mormon,' Mark said with a grin.

Duane offered a weak, half-hearted handshake, then led the way out of the coffee shop, muttering something about which casino they would be headed to first.

Morton sat back in his seat and exhaled, immediately ploughing back over their conversation and wondering if he had said enough, or if he'd been sufficiently convincing. It had certainly been a brief exchange, but one which he guessed he was lucky to have had at all. Sitting here in the wake of their discussion, it just didn't feel to him as though he'd pushed his points persuasively enough. He was certain that, as soon as they had left, Duane would have poured cold water all over any slight spark of interest that Mark had shown in the case.

Morton sighed again and said to himself, 'Well, it will be what it will be: *que será, será.*' He closed his laptop and packed his bag. It was time to fly to Salt Lake City.

Chapter Six

2nd March 2023, Salt Lake City, Utah, USA

Morton had found for himself a large empty table at the back
of the Expo Hall in the Salt Palace Convention Center, the host
location of the RootsTech conference. He told himself that the
fact that he was alone, sitting far from the next nearest occupied
tables, was because he wanted to have a final quiet run-through
of his *Researching Your Sussex Ancestors* presentation. The reality,
however, was that he was feeling incredibly overwhelmed by
the vastness of the building, the volume of people and the sheer
scale of the event itself. The thought of delivering his talk was
terrifying him. In just the first hour of the conference opening
this morning, over twenty lectures had been offered at the same
time. He had chosen *Comparing the Newspaper Giants* by Sunny
Morton, a name that he fancifully thought could be attributed
to him on one of his brighter days, though he knew that Juliette
would likely beg to differ. The talk was slick, interesting and
professional, which made him all the more anxious about his
own.

He reached the last slide in his presentation, rehearsed his
closing comments and took a long breath, noticing a lunchtime
influx around him. He eyed the growing queue at a food
concession just a few metres away, where various flavours of
rice bowls were being served from the side of a Sobe Eats
trailer. Although he wasn't feeling particularly hungry, he knew
that he should definitely eat before his talk. He stood up and
headed towards the food outlet.

He approached the A-frame board advertising the variety of
food on offer. *Sweet Carnitas. Chicken Tinga. Garlic Shrimp. Tuna
Poke.* He read the description for each bowl, beginning to feel

slightly peckish, when, out of his peripheral vision, he caught sight of someone that made his heart feel as though it had come to a sudden, juddering halt. Despite the complete absence of her in his life for many years, Morton knew that the figure, standing with her back to him and ordering her food, was Maddie.

They hadn't been in the same room for twenty-six years and now there she was, standing just two metres away from him. What should he do or say? Tap her on the shoulder, as if they were old friends? Mumble something about the situation being awkward? Ignore their past history altogether and discuss their panel talk tomorrow? Or perhaps make a joke to break the ice: Here you are! I've been looking everywhere for you for the last twenty-six years. Maybe not.

'Excuse me, are you in the line?' a voice asked from behind, startling him.

Morton turned to see a short lady, gesticulating towards the food trailer.

'Er, I think...' he answered. 'No. No, I'm not. Sorry.' Keeping his back to Maddie, he returned to his table, taking a surreptitious glance to the side as he went. She was still there, distracted by her mobile phone as she waited on her food.

Morton chanced a full look in her direction. It was a huge cliché—and one that he would not be sharing with Juliette—but Maddie really hadn't changed much in the intervening years: still had the same youthful face framed by shoulder-length blonde curly hair; still had the same slightly Bohemian style of dressing with ripped jeans and a baggy knitted jumper; and, he guessed, she still had the same fiery independence and determination that she'd always had.

Maddie unexpectedly looked up from her phone in his direction. Startled, Morton hurriedly looked down at his laptop and feigned being engrossed in his emails. Why was he being so ridiculous? It wasn't even as though he would be able to avoid her for the duration of the conference; he would literally be sitting on stage with her this same time tomorrow. He took a deep breath and turned to face her. But she was gone, striding away with her rice bowl in hand.

He felt like a complete idiot. Stupid is as stupid does, he reminded himself.

He was no longer feeling the slightest bit hungry. In fact, on the contrary, with just thirty-five minutes to go until his talk, he was feeling decidedly sick. He thought that the best thing to settle his nerves would be to go to the room where he would be delivering his talk and get himself mentally prepared for it.

As he was about to close his laptop, he saw that he had an email from Margot.

Hi Morton,

Hope your galivanting around America is going well. Juliette and I are managing to hold the fort at home. I popped back to my place yesterday with Grace and found the letter from Charles. She was interested in the story too – future career?! Anyway, hopefully it's attached, and you can read it?

Good luck with your talks.

Margot x

Morton clicked the attachment. He rolled his eyes when he saw that the photo of the letter, taken on Margot's kitchen floor, was very out of focus, while the patterned lino beneath it was helpfully crisp and sharp. Zooming in only emphasised the blurriness but, through squinting, strained eyes, he could just about read it.

Dear Allie,

This is Charles writing & I will tell you truthfully all the main things. The thing I have to say will be quite a surprise to you but the time has come when I must talk. So this letter here from now on will be mostly for Allie & also for my two dear children, Arthur and Laura.

I like a scoundrel left you and the children to fight it out. The driving power was like something behind you compelling you to do a thing you didn't want to do. Knowing what was the right thing to do & doing opposite. You can easily see that something is wrong to go off & leave a wife & two babies & I wasn't crazy. I don't think I will ever be able to make any one understand. I don't myself, all I am sure of was I did that which I didn't want to do and I am absolutely certain that I dug up the Devil himself in Ypres and no matter where I went he followed me around.

I found myself in Las Vegas and the Wild West, doing all kinds of wicked things in the Devil's name. But in the fall of 1929 Jesus Christ saved my soul & took sin & hardness out of my life. When the Lord was about to save me I told him about you & my life and all the dark deeds I had done & Christ let me know he could save even the uttermost as recorded in Isaiah 1:18 (Come now, and let us reason together, saith the Lord: though your sins be as scarlet, they shall be as white as snow; though they be red like crimson, they shall be as wool.) Now I have been born again and all things have changed. Smoking, drinking, swearing, prostitutes, lying & all manner of wickedness has left. After years in the wilderness I am removed from the Devil's grip and he is returned to the ground. I am now a regular at the Pentecostal Church.

Now according to God's word, Allie you are my wife & always will be as long as we live. "Romans 7: 2&3" (For the woman which hath a husband is bound by the law to her husband so long as he liveth; but if, while her husband liveth, she be married to another man, she shall be called an adulteress) but there is here in Prescott a Christian woman that I married & 6 children that God has to do something about. God will work out our troubles if we let Him.

Now Allie I am not expecting sympathy because I don't deserve it & perhaps this will be hard for you to understand but God has given me a heart of flesh in stead of a heart of stone & sure He has taken me & opened my eyes & I see differently now. I know a lot of harm has been done by my being so hounded by the Devil. I trust you will understand this letter as I mean it, I don't wear my collar backwards or am not funny. Jesus has washed away my sins & I am free of the chains of the Devil & desire above all to atone for all I have done so with this I leave the dicision in your hands as what you want to do.

According to God's word my place is with you & the children as your husband & their father. That dicision I have to leave with you whether you want me back or not.

May God bless you all.

Charles

P.S. If you haven't a bible borrow one & look up these verses.

'Wow,' Morton muttered to himself. The letter needed a lot of unpicking but now wasn't the right time. He closed his laptop, pushing the bizarre letter from his mind, and sauntered out of the huge Expo Hall.

He walked the vast main corridor to room 155D. An elderly lady with a bright blue jumper, ferociously sucking a sweet, stood up as he neared the door. 'There's a talk going on in there right now,' she whispered. 'Want to go in?'

Morton nodded. 'I'm in there next, presenting.'

The woman rearranged the sweet in her mouth and replied, 'Go right on in.' She pulled open the door and Morton stepped inside. The room was big, but not as large as some of the other monstrously large ballrooms that he had seen this morning. There was a good-sized crowd watching the presenter on stage and she was flanked by two screens displaying the presentation. Morton smiled. The presenter was his friend, Else Churchill, the Chief Genealogist from the British Society of Genealogists.

Morton sat back, listening to the talk about using the society's extensive library at a distance. For a moment, he forgot about his plaguing anxieties and simply enjoyed listening to Else, making a few notes about some new digitised records to explore at a later date.

When Else mentioned the raft of online talks, which the

society offered, Morton recalled a recent one that he had attended by Dr Sophie Kay on negative space in genealogy. She had given the interesting analogy of not assuming that, having pieced together a single cat in a jigsaw puzzle, the entire picture would therefore be full of cats. She asked the question why, in genealogy, would assumptions be made about an ancestor's whole life based only on a small number of evidence points. It was a very good and valid argument. Morton was guilty of ignoring the negative space in Charles Hughes's life. That small handful of years between 1918 and 1929 were crucial in Charles's story of his transition to becoming Roy Stewart. He needed to try to do more to establish what had happened to him and where he had been. Could he have been in Las Vegas in those eleven elusive interim years? He would try and find out. But not now. Now he was due to give his presentation. Else had finished and was descending the stairs from the stage.

Morton walked towards her with a confidence that he did not feel as a bi-directional flux of audience members left and entered the auditorium, with just a few minutes in which to locate their next chosen class. His nerves began to writhe inside him.

'Hi, Morton,' Else greeted, while having her headset microphone removed by a member of staff. 'It's really good to see you.'

'And you,' Morton replied. 'I enjoyed your talk. I need to set aside quite a bit of time to spend on the society's website by the sounds of things. There's loads going on.'

'Yes, we've got some cracking records on there,' Else said. 'Are you speaking next?'

Morton nodded. '*Researching Your Sussex Ancestors*,' he said.

'You've got quite a crowd gathering, by the looks,' she noted, nodding to the people taking their seats. 'You'll need to be getting up there. I think they're ready for you. Good luck.'

'Thanks,' he replied, making his way to the stage, where a waiting event attendant fitted his microphone.

He walked over to the podium, where another member of staff assisted him in loading up his presentation.

Morton took a deep breath and looked out at the audience, thinking there to be at least seventy people staring at him, with still more filing in. His eyes scanned forwards, mercifully not landing on anyone familiar, until… He looked at the front row. Maddie was sitting there cross-legged and smiling up at him.

Chapter Seven

'Wow,' Morton gasped. The room—*Ballroom B*—was even more huge than the one in which he had delivered his talk yesterday. He was standing in the lower concourse of the Salt Palace, peering into the space through the rear doors at the distant stage where he was going to be delivering his panel talk in just over one hour's time.

'Pretty big, huh?' someone said, arriving alongside him.

He turned to his side to see the American DNA expert, Diahan Southard, smiling at him. 'Hi,' he said, extending his hand to her. 'I'm Morton Farrier. I'm a panellist with you later. And yes, it is very big. *Very*.'

'It's great to meet you,' she said, shaking his hand. 'It should be really interesting and fun. Are you ready for it?'

'Yes. And no,' he answered, somewhat vaguely. Although his genetic genealogy presentation was at last finished, he had yet to go through it again in its entirety. 'What about you?'

'Yeah, I think so,' she said with a nod. 'I've got like seven presentations and they're all pretty well there.'

'Seven?' Morton replied. 'That's impressive. Apart from this genetic genealogy one we're about to do, I came over from England just to deliver the one that I did yesterday on researching Sussex ancestors. That was enough for me.'

'Cool. And how did that go?'

He reflected for a moment on the talk, then answered, 'Surprisingly well, actually.' The presentation had run smoothly and perfectly to time, with laughter, nodding heads and the jotting down of key information in all the right places. He'd even managed to rise above the distracting fact that Maddie had been sitting in the front row. She had lingered to one side after the presentation had ended, but he had had a small queue of people wanting to discuss research in Sussex and, so, she hadn't waited and instead slipped away before he could speak with her. They were literally going to be meeting one another again for the first time in twenty-six years, on a stage and in front of a live, in-person and virtual audience.

'That's great. You can relax and get to enjoy RootsTech after this one. Nice to meet you,' Diahan said.

'Yes, and you,' he responded. 'See you back here in a little while.'

'Bye,' she said, walking off before turning back and adding, 'You do know the room won't get any smaller the longer you stare at it, right?'

Morton grinned at her correct intuition; the vastness of the room was indeed daunting. He closed the ballroom door and looked down the long corridor, spotting a coffee concession a short distance away. Maybe caffeine wouldn't be the best thing to settle his nerves, but he went ahead and ordered one anyway, convincing himself somehow that it would help.

He carried the coffee over to a quieter area with seating and opened up his laptop, intending to go through his presentation. But he just couldn't help himself and simply had to reread Charles Hughes's letter that was still open on-screen.

The part that struck Morton the most was Charles's insistence that the devil had been behind his decision to abandon his wife and children and the root cause of all the bad things to which he had confessed in his letter. One phrase in particular drew Morton's attention: *I am absolutely certain that I dug up the Devil himself in Ypres.* Was this, as it seemed to be, a reference to his service in the First World War? What on earth could have happened to the man?

Morton drank some coffee, then ran a Google search for the Royal Engineers, finding that, among the many different units of which it had been comprised, one had been a tunnelling company for underground warfare. When he delved more deeply into their history, Morton found that they had indeed served at Ypres, building and then exploding tunnels beneath enemy trenches. Could this be what Charles had been referring to? Had the horrors that he had witnessed on and below the battlefields of the Western Front manifested in his mind as the devil, which would today probably be labelled as PTSD. A dark incarnation that Charles had felt compelled to cross the Atlantic to try and evade? Maybe. A definitive answer to this question was very likely long lost to history.

The next paragraph was the only one that intimated what might have occurred during those eleven years of negative space. *I found myself in Las Vegas and the Wild West...* Did any documentation exist that would offer a glimpse into Charles Hughes's life there?

Morton saved the blurred letter to Charles Hughes's family tree profile—intending to obtain a better, focused copy when he got back home—then closed it and went through his presentation slides for the first and final time before he would be due on stage.

'Okay,' he mumbled to himself, folding away his laptop and finishing his coffee. Thankfully, the caffeine had helped. He walked back towards the rear doors of the ballroom, then faltered, wondering if he'd gone to the incorrect location. A queue of at least fifty people was slowly drifting into the room.

'Sorry, sorry. Excuse me,' Morton kept apologising, as he had to push his way to the front of the long line. 'I'm one of the panellists. Sorry.'

Finally, he made it inside the room. At least two hundred people were already seated. Was he late? he wondered, rushing to the front. Diahan Southard, Roberta Estes and Jonny Perl were already seated, all chatting nonchalantly to each other and the host, Drew Smith.

Yes, he was late. But then again, so was Maddie. Maybe she wasn't coming, he thought hopefully as he hurried up the short flight of steps and onto the stage.

'Hello, sorry,' he greeted the group.

Drew Smith faced him with a warm smile. 'Morton Farrier, I don't believe we've ever met.'

'No, we haven't,' Morton answered, 'but I feel as though we have because I listen to *The Genealogy Guys Podcast*.'

Drew smiled. 'And have you met your co-panellists?' he asked, stepping back and gesturing to Roberta, Diahan and Jonny.

The reality and gravity of his situation suddenly dawned on Morton as he found himself facing three of the biggest names in the genealogy world. How had he ended up here? 'Diahan and I go way back,' Morton began, overcompensating and intending to make a comical reference to their having first met just a short while ago, but then Drew's and his co-panellists' attention shifted to the person who had just sat down beside Morton with a giant sigh: Maddie.

'Hi,' Morton said, his voice catching in his throat. But his greeting was lost in the mêlée of other voices.

'Hi, everyone,' Maddie said, smiling and nodding down the line. 'Good to see you again, Diahan.'

'And you,' she replied with a warm smile.

If Morton hadn't seen Maddie at his talk yesterday, or had the brief email exchange about the Candee-Lee Gaddy case, then he might well have believed from the way in which she was interacting with him that she had entirely obliterated any residual memory of their former shared life together.

Morton's mobile vibrated in his pocket. It was on silent, but he wanted it switched off completely for the presentation. He pulled it out to see that it was a text from Juliette. Morton's blood ran cold as he read the message.

Good luck! The kids are in bed and mum and I are ready to watch the live-stream! So exciting!! Xx

'Two minutes to live,' a member of staff wearing a headset

announced at the edge of the stage. At that moment, a large video camera slowly arced in on a jib arm above the assembled audience, which by now numbered several hundred.

'Good luck,' Drew said to them all, heading over to the lectern and looking into the camera in anticipation of his cue.

Morton switched off his mobile phone and swallowed as he looked numbly out at the audience.

A red light above the camera began to flash.

'Thirty seconds to live,' someone announced.

Morton took in a long breath and looked at his co-panellists, who, unlike him, all seemed completely relaxed and at ease.

The red light began to flash furiously.

'Five seconds to live.'

The red light went solid.

'Hello, my name is Drew Smith and I'd like to welcome in-person and virtual attendees to this live RootsTech presentation, entitled *Genetic Genealogy: some recent case studies*. As you can see, behind me sit some of the top people working in this field today. They all come from different spheres and even different parts of the globe, but they are all unified in being experts in genetic genealogy. I am delighted to welcome Roberta Estes, Morton Farrier, Madison Scott-Barnhart, Jonny Perl and Diahan Southard here to share with you some case studies in genetic genealogy.'

The audience clapped enthusiastically, and Morton wondered what on earth Juliette must be thinking right now, this being the first time that she would have heard that he was sharing the stage with Maddie, who was sitting right beside him with a fixed smile on her face. Morton cringed internally to hear their names together like that. The last time anyone had read their names aloud together had probably been at University College London, when Maddie had appeared on an exchange programme from the US. Morton's Photo Forensics lecturer, Dr Baumgartner, had put them together to work on a project that had been the catalyst for their ensuing relationship.

Another round of applause unstitched Morton's thoughts from his memories.

Roberta Estes stood up and walked over to the lectern. 'Good afternoon,' she began, clicking to move her presentation to the first slide. The two giant screens that framed the stage changed to a sepia photograph of a serious-looking man with glasses and a cap, leaning on the open driver's door of an old American car. 'November third, 1956,' Roberta began. 'This man is in a car accident that nearly kills him. Police come and take his wife and daughter to the hospital, telling them that he wasn't expected to live. A few hours later, another woman, also with a young child hurried into the hospital room, looking for her husband. The first woman motioned helpfully to the next bed, but the visitor returned and said, 'No, *this* man is my husband.' Both women stared at each other and their babies, incredulous as the awful truth slowly sank in.'

Morton craned his neck as the slide changed to a black-and-white photograph of the same man, sitting in front of a large window with a child upon his lap.

'That man was a serial bigamist and the little girl in his lap—the one initially waiting at the hospital with her mother—well, that was me.'

Given the case that Morton had found himself now inadvertently researching, Roberta Estes's talk thoroughly gripped him. She talked about how she had eventually come to know her new half-sibling—the other child present at the hospital—only to have DNA conclude that they were in fact not related at all; the other wife had been cheating on *him*, and the child had not been biologically his.

Morton listened with intent, his brain jumping from questions that he had for Roberta; to conjecturing about Charles Hughes; to considering what on earth Juliette might be thinking about this ex-girlfriend of his, seated cosily beside him.

The audience was clapping appreciatively, and Drew Smith was back at the lectern. 'Wow,' he said. 'What a fascinating story, Roberta. Thank you. Up next, presenting *his* genetic genealogy case study for us, is Morton Farrier.'

Out of nowhere, Maddie patted his thigh, making Morton tense up even more before he'd even begun the presentation. Would Juliette have just seen that? he wondered. He stood up and walked over to the front of the stage, clearing his throat before he reached the microphone. He stared nervously out at the audience as the camera on the jib arm slowly travelled in towards him.

'Good afternoon, everyone,' he started, clicking his first slide. 'Candee-Lee Gaddy, a twenty-three-year-old prostitute from Reno was brutally murdered in December 1980.' He craned his neck to check that the grainy photograph taken from the *Reno Evening Gazette* was being projected on the giant screen behind him. It was. 'The case then went cold until 2019, when investigative genetic genealogy identified the killer.' Morton smiled and turned briefly to Maddie. 'Actually, I should add that it was my co-presenter's company, Venator, that identified the killer. The person that they identified and named posthumously was this man.' Morton clicked the slide on to a photograph of an old man, wearing a flat cap, standing proudly in a vegetable garden with his foot upon a spade, and smiling into the camera. 'His name was Alfred Farrier, and he was my grandfather.'

There was a collective gasp from the audience and Morton knew that he now had their full attention. With a newfound sense of confidence, Morton retold the complicated story of Rosie Hart, her abandoned children, and his own theories about the possible murders that she had committed.

His presentation ended with details of his meeting two days ago with the detectives in Las Vegas, who were considering reopening the investigation into Candee-Lee's murder. 'And, sorry, to my friend here,' he said, again referring to Maddie with a smile, 'but I hope to use genetic genealogy again, this time to exonerate my grandfather.'

The audience clapped and Morton made his way back to his

seat, berating himself for referring to Maddie as his friend. If the whole thing hadn't been so cringe-worthy, he might have watched the presentation back to see exactly how it would have looked from Juliette's perspective.

'Well, best of luck with that, Morton,' Drew said to the audience with a chuckle. 'Next up, we have Madison Scott-Barnhart, who—and I'm hoping here—*isn't* going to be talking about the Candee-Lee Gaddy case!'

The audience laughed and then applauded as Maddie walked over to the lectern.

'No, I won't be talking about that case,' she said with a chuckle. 'Imagine that. Although…my team and I would be very happy to handle the DNA analysis for you in this part of the investigation,' she said, turning to Morton.

He grinned up at her, every moment of the embarrassing exchange increasing the awkwardness that he was feeling inside.

'Where Morton and Roberta have spoken about cases close to home, I will *definitely* not be; I will be talking about *this* man,' she said, clicking on a slide that displayed the infamous police mugshot of Dexter Beynon. 'The man my team and I identified as the Winterset Butcher, using investigative genetic genealogy.'

Morton sat through Maddie's presentation with what he hoped projected an interested face but, at the same time, one that Juliette wouldn't read as appearing overly keen. Maddie's talk was slick and professional, summarising with clarity and precision the whole process of investigative genetic genealogy and how the Venator team finally gave a name to the man who had butchered at least nine victims between 1979 and 1984 in Iowa.

The audience applauded as Maddie returned to her seat. 'How'd I do?' she whispered.

'Great,' Morton replied enthusiastically.

'Okay, thank you very much, Maddie. That's one less bad guy on the streets,' Drew Smith said. 'And, next up, we have a man who has given the genetic genealogy community a whole raft of amazing third-party tools through his DNA Painter website: it's Jonny Perl.'

'Thank you,' Jonny began, once his applause had simmered down. 'Well—just to manage your expectations—although my talk is about an aspect of my own family tree, it does not include serial killers or bigamists.' There was a ripple of laughter before he continued. 'I'm going to be speaking about my father's German Jewish heritage and the impact of endogamy on genetic genealogy. I'll then suggest some strategies that those who are working with endogamous ancestry might find helpful.'

Although Morton had so far not discovered any endogamy in his family tree, the presentation was extremely interesting, and he tried to commit several new techniques to memory, which he would be able to apply to his work as a forensic genealogist for other people.

Jonny took his seat as the audience showed their appreciation for his talk.

'Thank you very much,' Drew said, taking over the microphone once more. 'We really appreciate all the DNA tools that you've brought to our community. Our final talk—before we then open up the floor to your questions for the panel—comes from the DNA guru, Diahan Southard.'

Diahan waited at the lectern for the applause to subside, then said with a wry smile, 'I also will not be talking about murderers, but rather a truly wonderful and emotional story that came out of my DNA Skills workshop.'

Morton listened, fascinated by the story of two enslaved siblings who were sold to separate families in different states and how the descendants of one of the siblings had used genetic genealogy to reconnect finally with descendants of her ancestor's brother.

Just as Diahan had said, the story of separation and reuniting was wonderful and also surprisingly emotional, and Morton was forced to fight back the tears.

'Okay,' Drew said, clearing his throat and tapping his chest. 'That was a very touching story, thank you. As genealogists, I tend to think those kinds of stories resonate with us on a whole other level. Right... We're now going to open to a few questions from the audience. Raise your hands and we'll try and get a microphone over to you.'

Many hands instantly shot up around the room and Drew fielded questions, some for specific presenters and some generic for each of them to voice their opinions, one after the other. Finally, the session was over and that accusing red light above the camera went dark.

Morton exhaled loudly.

'That was a big sigh,' Maddie said, standing up.

'Just glad it's over and done with,' Morton lied in reply. He could hardly tell her that his wife would have been watching live from home, completely unprepared and unaware that his ex-girlfriend would be sitting next to him.

Drew thanked the panel and they all said goodbye to one another, the general agreement being that the session had gone down very well with the audience.

When it was just the two of them left on stage, Maddie asked, 'Do you wanna get some lunch?'

Morton nodded. 'Sure,' he answered, uncertain of the wisdom of that response.

'There's a great place close to my work, called Eva's Bakery. They do an amazing brunch flatbread: eggs, cheese, smoked ham and hollandaise. It's the best.'

'Sounds great.'

Chapter Eight

3rd March 2023, Salt Lake City, Utah, USA

Morton was sitting opposite Maddie in Eva's Bakery on Main Street, Salt Lake City. The place was a delightful French-style boulangerie, specialising in continental breads and cakes. They were tucked just behind the counter at a small, round, Parisian-style table, awaiting their food order.

'I forgot how much you liked your coffee,' Maddie noted with a smile, holding her own drink between her two hands.

'*You* can talk,' he replied, remembering how much filter coffee they both would get through when they had lived together.

'It was a long time ago,' she muttered.

Morton gazed into her green eyes, wondering if she was experiencing the same rekindling of their shared past. He took her in fully for the first time in twenty-six years, wondering what had happened to the feelings that they had once had for one another; or at least, the ones that he had had for her. He recalled the night that he had first said that he loved her. They'd gone out in London for a drink to celebrate their final university exams. One drink had turned into several and, in the corner of a dingy nightclub, called The Cow & Staple, he had whispered that he loved her. He'd been wanting to say it for some time, but the words would never push through the fear that she might not have reciprocated. However, she had reciprocated, telling him that she'd felt it for a long time but also hadn't been able to vocalise her feelings.

'What are you thinking about?' Maddie asked.

'Oh, nothing,' he replied, then took a sip of coffee and gave a half-truthful answer. 'I was thinking about The Cow & Staple.' He knew that she would fully understand to what he was inferring.

She offered a thin smile. 'God, that was a whole different lifetime,' she mused.

Morton wanted to press her on the reason that she had suddenly walked out on him with no explanation. Instead, though, he simply murmured his agreement.

'What was the name of our favourite lecturer, again? Doctor someone.'

'Dr Baumgartner,' he answered.

Maddie clicked her fingers. 'Dr Baumgartner, that's it. He was a great teacher. I wonder what ever happened to him.'

'Oh, I think he's retired now. But a few years ago, he actually helped me on a genealogical case that I was working on.' Morton grinned. 'Actually, the first genetic genealogy case that I worked on, although it wasn't called that back then. I say a few years ago… It'll be ten years in September.'

'2013? That's very early for genetic genealogy in the UK,' Maddie commented. 'What was the case?'

'Proving that an eight-year-old boy was related to an English aristocratic family, who wanted to deny that they were related. Swabbed the boy, took a trash DNA sample and had Dr Baumgartner test it at the Forensic Science Service,' Morton summarised.

Maddie frowned. 'Is that even legal in the UK?'

Morton shook his head.

'And ethically, you're okay with that?' Maddie asked, unable to conceal the incredulity from her voice.

'Now, no,' Morton replied. 'Back then, yes. I've changed,' he admitted. '*Maybe* even finally grown up a bit.'

'We're trying to make investigative genetic genealogy more rigorous and disciplined over here,' Maddie said. 'That kind of thing would *not* go down at all well amidst the arguments that the industry is totally unregulated.'

'I know. I wouldn't do it now,' he insisted.

Maddie was about to speak when a waitress arrived at the

table, carrying their food. 'I see you've persuaded your friend to try the brunch flatbreads, Maddie,' the waitress said, setting the plates down in front of them.

Maddie opened her hands upwards. 'What can I say? It's simply the best.'

'Enjoy,' the waitress said, heading back to the counter.

'They know you by name in here?' Morton asked, picking up the flatbread and taking a big bite.

Maddie shrugged. 'My office is literally right across the street, so my team and I are in here all the time. Do you like it?'

'It's really nice,' Morton confirmed. 'Can I see your office? It would be good to get a feel for how all this investigative genetic genealogy works over here—with suspect cases and unidentified remains, I mean. I so wish we did it in the UK but we're a bit behind the times on all that.'

'Sure, it would be great to show you around,' Maddie agreed. 'We can go after this if you're free?'

'Great.'

They ate in a very strangely comfortable silence, although Morton couldn't help wondering if she too was pondering whether or not to address their elephant in the room. Should he just come right out and ask why she had walked out on him with nothing more than a short note and no explanation? Or did she think that, given the amount of time that had passed and the lives which they had created independently of one another, that meant that the ending of the relationship was nothing more than a minor footnote in the wholeness of their lives?

Morton raked back over the memories of the days and weeks after she had walked out. He wondered what had happened to his love for her. Had it died instantly? Or slowly faded to nothing? Or was it superseded by the love that he now felt for Juliette? One thing was certain, being with her now, he felt nothing at all romantically; just a long-held, forgotten desire to understand better what had happened.

He finished his flatbread, took the last mouthful of coffee and blurted it out. 'Maddie, why did you leave?' He realised that he sounded accusatory, which he supposed he was, but he added, 'Not that it matters now. I'd just really like to know. I've always felt that I should know the reason.'

Maddie finished her mouthful of food, staring beyond him as she chewed. She exhaled at length, then responded to the question with an answer that he'd waited twenty-six years to hear. 'I guess it was like you just said about yourself: I was young and didn't know how to handle a break-up. Rushing back home to the States just felt like the right thing to do at the time.' She sighed again, before echoing his words, 'I wouldn't do it now.'

She hadn't answered the question. 'But what made you want to leave?' he pushed. 'I had literally no idea you were unhappy, never mind *that* unhappy.'

'It was complicated, and it was a long time ago, Morton,' she replied. 'Does it matter, now? Aren't you happily married with kids?'

He shrugged and nodded. Did it matter now? In the grand scheme of his life, no, it didn't matter at all. Yet, still, the question lingered. If she knew him at all, she would know that he hated unanswered questions. 'Yes, I'm very happily married with two kids. And no, I guess it doesn't matter…beyond curiosity. Like you wanting to know what happened to Dr Baumgartner.' He shrugged again. 'Maybe it's the inquisitive genealogist in me that doesn't like loose ends.'

'Loose ends?' Maddie questioned.

'You know what I mean.'

'What do you want me to say, Morton? A life in England, living in a small flat with you, thousands of miles from my family just wasn't what I wanted.'

And right there was his answer. The life that he had been able to offer her at the time simply hadn't been enough. 'You could have told me how you felt.'

'Yes, I could have,' she replied. 'And I should have. But what would it have changed?'

Now the silence that lingered between them shifted to being uncomfortable. But he had an answer of sorts. There was nothing to be gained by pursuing it any further. 'So, you married and had kids yourself?'

Maddie visibly brightened. 'Yeah, that's right. I've got two in college and one who lives down in Florida, although she's back here on vacation at the moment. She's a forensic anthropologist, so we both spend more time working with the dead than the living.'

Morton smiled. 'My dad's a forensic archaeologist and works all around the US—maybe they might know one another.'

'Your dad?' she asked incredulously, clearly not able to link this sentence to the man whom she had known from her time in England.

'Oh, yeah. Sorry. My *biological* father,' he revealed.

'Wow, that's amazing,' Maddie said. 'When we were together, you were very much against finding out. Tell me more.'

And so, Morton spent some time explaining how he had gone from the adoptee, whom she had known, with no idea about his biological identity, to the person who now knew rather a lot more about his heritage.

'So, your dad's *American*. Amazing. What's his name?' She asked.

'Harley Jacklin, known as Jack,' Morton answered.

'Unreal. That's fantastic. Good for you,' Maddie said. 'And you have a relationship with him?'

Morton nodded. 'Yeah, obviously we don't see each other that often but we chat and email a lot.'

'Amazing.'

The waitress returned to the table. 'Did you like it?' she asked Morton.

'Really good, thank you very much,' he answered, before

turning to Maddie. 'I can see why you come here so often.'

The waitress smiled and cleared their plates. 'Can I get you guys anything else?'

'Oh, I'm nicely full up, thank you,' Morton replied.

'We're good, thank you. I'll just get the check,' Maddie said, and the waitress left them again. 'Then you can come over to the office to see where all the magic happens.'

'Great,' he said, sliding his mobile phone from his pocket and taking out his credit card from the cover. As he did so, he realised that his phone was still switched off from the panel presentations. He turned it back on and saw that he had several missed calls from Juliette. Twelve, to be precise. So, she'd watched the presentation, then.

'I'll get this,' Maddie said, handing the waitress some dollar bills when she returned.

'Oh… Thank you.'

Maddie stood up and tucked her chair under the table. 'You ready?'

Morton nodded. 'I just need to make a quick call. Sorry. You go ahead and I'll follow on in a moment. Where am I headed?' he asked, unable to recall the specific address on this street from his email communication with her four years ago.

'It's the Kearns Building, the tall one right across the street. We're on the fifth floor. See you in a minute.'

Morton nodded and slowly walked out of the bakery into the afternoon sunshine. He stood out on the wide Main Street pavement under a bare tree, watching Maddie cross the two lanes of vehicle traffic and tram lines to walk the short distance into an elegant, historic-looking building. It was a ten-storey, cream-coloured, brick structure that sat slightly incongruously with the more modern glass-fronted US Bank beside it.

Morton opened the call log on his mobile phone. At the top of the *Recents* list was Juliette with the number twelve in brackets. His finger lingered over her name as he wondered what on earth he was going to say that didn't sound evasive or defensive and make him appear guilty of something that he hadn't actually done. He lightly kicked at a pile of dirty snow at the side of the pavement, then took the plunge and tapped her name.

She answered after one ring. 'Oh, at last,' she said. 'I've tried ringing like twenty times.'

'Twelve, actually,' he corrected.

'If I hadn't just seen you live, I might have got worried. I just wanted to say well done. That was an amazing presentation. All of you were brilliant. Even my mum was impressed.'

'Oh,' Morton responded, unable to conceal his surprise.

'Bet that was a bit of a shock being on stage with Maddie, wasn't it?'

'Just slightly. And very awkward. I've just had lunch with her, actually,' he said with a grimace, suddenly keen to tell her everything.

'How did that go?'

Morton at last regained a normal breathing rhythm. Juliette was taking all of this exceptionally well. Or perhaps he had been pre-judging her based on how he would have reacted were the situation reversed. 'Alright, I suppose. I asked why she left me twenty-six years ago.' In for a penny, he thought.

Juliette laughed. 'Because you're weird?'

'Well, she didn't say that explicitly, no. Apparently, she just didn't want to live in a small flat with me so far away from her family. She wanted more.'

'Ah, poor Morton. Good job I came along when I did, then,' she said with another laugh.

'And I wouldn't change it for the world,' he said, suddenly feeling emotional. 'I'm really missing you all, even your mum the tiniest bit.'

'Only three days until you're home again,' Juliette said.

Morton smiled, feeling a deep warmth inside at the thought of being back at The House with Two Front Doors with his wife and two children. 'How are you all?'

'Same as usual, I think,' she answered. 'What are you up to, now that your talks are all done?'

'Maddie's about to give me a tour of her office, then I'm going back to the hotel to crack on with your great-grandfather's case.'

'Oh, yeah? You didn't think you'd have time for that. How's it going?'

'Interestingly, to be fair... I'll tell you everything properly when I get home.'

'Sounds intriguing,' she said.

'He certainly lived an *interesting* life,' Morton confirmed. 'Listen. I have to catch her up. I sent her on ahead, so I could call you.'

'Sure. Okay. You go. Love you, bye.'

'Love you, too.' Morton ended the call and felt a weight lift from his shoulders. What had he done to deserve her? Whatever Maddie's reasons had been for leaving him the way that she had, his life now proved to him that it had actually been one of the best things that could have happened to him.

Pocketing his mobile phone, he crossed the street and made his way to the Kearns Building. As he approached the entrance, the gold-trimmed, glass front door opened automatically, and he stepped inside a warm lobby with a tiled floor. He moved further inside, spotting the staircase running up beside three elevators.

Just as he was deciding which to take, the nearest elevator pinged an arrival alert and a young woman, who seemed vaguely familiar, stepped out.

'You want this?' she asked, stepping back quickly to hold the door open.

'I'm not sure, actually,' he said, dithering. 'I'm going up to the Venator office and can't decide whether to walk or take the lift.'

The woman grinned. 'That's my mom's company. It's on the fifth floor. So, unless you want to arrive breathless, I'd take the elevator.'

'Okay, decision made,' Morton replied, stepping towards it and taking her in fully now that he knew who she was. She was in her mid-twenties, pretty, with dark brown eyes and her mother's crazy blonde hair. 'I used to know your mother many years ago. I'm an old friend,' he said whilst entering the lift.

'Ah, that's cool,' she replied. 'Well, it was nice to meet you.'

'And you,' he called, as the closing doors ended their interaction for them.

The lift to the fifth floor seemed to take an age and Morton was glad that he had not taken the stairs. He walked a short distance and came to an office door with a frosted glass window and, below that, a brass plaque that read, *VENATOR. INVESTIGATIVE GENETIC GENEALOGY.*

Morton opened the door and stepped into a small reception area. A young man with a mop of blond hair looked up and smiled. 'Morton?'

'Yeah. That's me,' he replied.

'Ross,' he introduced, extending his hand as he stood up. 'Nice to meet you.'

'You, too,' Morton replied, shaking his hand.

'Maddie's expecting you,' Ross said. 'I'll show you to her office.'

'Thanks,' Morton replied, following the young man through an open-plan office in which several people were seated working at computers, through a small kitchenette to an office with an open door. Maddie was sitting at the room's only desk, typing something into a computer.

'Hey,' she said, glancing up. 'Give me twenty seconds to get this email out.'

'No worries,' Morton answered, looking around the room at the bulging bookshelves which reminded him of his own study at home. On her desk was an assortment of seemingly haphazard paperwork, two empty mugs and some framed photographs that he surreptitiously tried to see.

Without taking her eyes from her computer screen, Maddie picked up each photograph in turn and held it towards him. 'Michael—husband. Jenna—eldest. Nikki and Trenton— adopted from South Korea.'

'So… I just met Jenna, then,' Morton replied.

Maddie's eyes flicked quickly towards him. 'What?'

'I just met Jenna downstairs in the lobby. She advised taking the lift over walking up, and from the time it took, I think she was right.'

'Oh, right,' Maddie said, standing from her desk. 'Ready for a tour? It won't take long; we literally have this one space.'

Morton followed her out into the open-plan office. The room was spacious but dominated by three six-foot-wide boards at the front of the room. One appeared to be a digital whiteboard, sandwiched between a glass writing board and a regular whiteboard. Each was brimming with information, maps, post-it notes and photographs.

'What are you working on at the moment?' he asked.

Maddie grimaced. 'I can't tell you that. It's quite a high-profile one.'

'Intriguing,' he mumbled, trying to take a subtle look at the content of the investigation boards which resembled a scene from CSI. On the digital whiteboard was a map zoomed in to a large body of water, which someone had annotated with the words *LAKE MEAD*. On the whiteboard, written in red were four names and, below each, were photographs and information too small for him to glean. And on the glass writing board, a large family tree had been hand-drawn.

'Morton. I can see what you're doing,' Maddie said. 'Stop trying to figure out what our case is! Come on. Come meet my team. This is Kenyatta, my wonderful deputy.'

A middle-aged African American lady stood up and, with a smile, offered her hand to shake. 'Nice to meet you, Morton. So, you and Maddie go back a long way, huh?'

'Yes, that's right. It seems a lifetime ago, back in England in

1995. She waltzed into my Photo Forensics Lecture like an American tornado, whipping everyone up.'

Kenyatta grinned and folded her arms. 'Is that so? Funny. She never talked about her time in England before. You and I should chat some more.' She looked at Maddie inquisitively.

'Okay, you two. Moving on,' Maddie said, directing him over to where a young woman with glasses and mousey hair was sitting at a computer, studying a photograph of what appeared to be a large wooden barrel. 'Becky, this is my friend from England, Morton. Morton, Becky.'

'Hi, there,' she said, shaking his hand. She did a double take from Maddie back to him. 'Morton as in Morton Farrier?'

Morton smiled, impressed that he was becoming known internationally. 'Yep, that's me.'

Becky looked at Maddie again. 'Candy-Lee-Gaddy Morton Farrier?'

'Yeah, that's him,' Maddie confirmed.

'Oh,' Becky replied, clearly taken aback. 'So, what brings you to Salt Lake?'

'RootsTech, actually,' Morton replied, aware that he was blushing. 'I did a couple of presentations.'

'Cool,' Becky said. 'You know, even though it's right on my doorstep, I haven't actually managed to attend a single lecture. I'll catch them online afterward.'

'She just got back from her honeymoon, so she's playing catch up on her work,' Maddie explained.

'Ah, congratulations. That's lovely,' Morton said.

'Thanks,' she said, flashing her wedding ring.

'And last, but by no means least, this young man over here, working diligently as ever, is Reggie.'

An African American man in his twenties stood up and shook Morton's hand. 'Good to meet you, man.'

'Good to meet you, too. What are you diligently working on?' Morton asked.

'Don't tell him,' Maddie quickly instructed. 'He's fishing.

Nice try, Morton.'

'It's okay. I'm only pretending to work, anyway,' Reggie replied with a grin. 'I'm on TikTok, really.'

Maddie shrugged. 'You see what I have to put up with.'

'It must be great having a team around you,' Morton mused. 'I do like working alone but, just sometimes, I'd like to have colleagues to bounce ideas around with.'

'And people to fetch coffee and brunch flatbreads,' Maddie added.

'Exactly,' he replied. 'So, how do you divide up the work, so you don't end up repeating someone else's work?'

'Everyone here has their own skill sets and talents,' Maddie began, then stopped herself. 'Let me fix us some coffee and I'll tell you all about it, if you'd like?'

'Sounds great,' he replied, following Maddie over to the kitchenette where she poured two mugs of filter coffee. Back in her office, she talked to him at length about the Venator team and how they handle the investigative genetic genealogy cases that they take on.

They chatted for more than an hour, with Maddie happily showing him case files which had been successfully resolved.

'So, do you have a lot of cases running at the moment?' Morton asked.

Maddie nodded. 'Hell, yeah. We've got a lot that are just sitting and waiting for a decent DNA match to drop in. Plus, there's the pro bono work for the National Center for Missing and Exploited Children and working through cases that come our way from the backlog of sexual assault kits. We do all of that around the bigger cases that we usually work on as a team together.'

'Wow,' Morton said, impressed. 'I think I've figured out the one you're working on now. It even made the news in the UK.'

Maddie winked but said nothing.

'So, coming back to my grandfather's case again. If I had maybe, sort of, possibly hinted to the two cold-case detectives from Reno that I could get the IGG work done on the knife blade blood for free...' Morton grimaced, leaving his statement hanging in the air.

Maddie smiled. 'I'm sure we could work something out. It's important to put it right.'

'Oh, thanks, Maddie,' he said. 'Well, I'm conscious of how much of your time I've taken up... I guess I'd better leave you to it and explore the city a bit, since I've come all this way. I might hire one of those scooters that I see randomly discarded all over the place.'

'Oh, God. Don't do that,' she warned. 'You'll wind up in the hospital.'

Morton laughed as he stood up and headed towards the door. Maddie followed him out to the elevator and then hugged him.

'Listen, it was so good to catch up, Morton,' she said warmly. 'I really mean that.'

'Yeah, it was lovely to get to see you, too, Maddie,' he agreed.

'I expect our paths will cross from time to time now that you're on the international stage,' Maddie said with a grin.

'We'll see,' he replied. 'Goodbye. Take care.'

'Bye.'

Morton stepped into the lift and rode down to the ground floor, as a curious calmness settled inside him. Although the chapter of his life with Maddie had long since closed, he could now firmly bolt the door shut with everything inside resolved.

Morton left the Kearns Building with ideas to slowly wander the city. He only made it a few metres before being enticed by the culinary smells wafting from the neighbouring building, The BeerHive Pub. After the day he'd had, a drink was easily more enticing than exploration.

He entered the long and narrow pub, surprised at how busy the place was. A bar ran almost the entire length of the building, with tables and booths on the opposite side.

Finding a space at the bar, Morton ordered a local, honey

wheat beer and a BeerHive burger. Whilst he waited, he pulled up his emails. Among the usual dross and nonsense were two MyHeritage message notifications. One was from Bernadette Honeychurch, the other from Edie Loveless. Morton clicked to read Bernadette's message first.

Hey, Morton. Great to hear from you. Yes! Roy Stewart was my grandfather. I'm guessing your wife descends via the English family that we heard about? The poor first wife who died in childbirth? I remember hearing all about how cut up he was when he returned to England to find his kids had been taken away and even given new names. He used to tell us the stories of how he left England to find work in the U.S. It all affected him real bad, let me tell you. My father and his five siblings did not have the best time growing up. Do you have any information on his time in England? I'd love to know more. My cousin tried to find stuff out a few years ago but couldn't find any trace of him and we wondered if he'd actually made up his whole life in England! Excited to find out about him. Regards, Bernie

Oh, dear. Bernie was going to be in for a small shock when she found out about Roy's previous life as Charles Hughes.

Morton next clicked to read the message from Edie Loveless.

Thanks for contacting me. I'm a granddaughter from his marriage to Louise Bullington. I live in Las Vegas and would be happy to exchange information. Edie.

Morton read the message several times over. Who was Louise Bullington?

Chapter Nine

4th March 2023, Salt Lake City, Utah, USA

Morton walked out of the Salt Palace, carrying two bags full of DNA kits from all of the major genealogy companies, unable to resist the heavily discounted products. It was useful to have a good supply in stock for his case work, which increasingly involved genetic genealogy.

The skies above the city were ominously dark grey and he had overheard several people talking about an imminent snowstorm that was due. Although he'd loved his time here and at RootsTech, he hoped to goodness that his flight back to Las Vegas this evening wouldn't be delayed or cancelled because of the inclement weather. He had work to do and he was missing his family.

Morton pulled his jacket tight, braced against the plummeting temperatures. He strode the short distance to the FamilySearch Library, entering the warm building with some relief. As he might have expected with a place which boasted the largest collection of genealogical materials in the world, the building was huge, their records spread across five large floors. Genealogical heaven, he thought, looking around with a grin on his face like a child at Christmas. If there was one place in the world where he might stand a chance of filling in the eleven years of negative space in Charles Hughes's, aka Roy Stewart's, life, then it would be here. Except he only had six hours until he would need to leave for the airport to fly back to Las Vegas. Knowing how genealogy was notoriously capable of warping his grip on time, Morton had set an alarm on his phone to remind him when it was time to stop and leave.

The first step that he needed to take today was to try and find documentation that would corroborate what Edie Loveless had stated in her message about a marriage to a Louise Bullington. He had replied straight away, requesting any further information and asking if she would be able to meet him tomorrow in Las Vegas before he was due to fly back home. Despite repeatedly checking his MyHeritage messages, she still had not answered him. He had also not heard back as yet from Bernadette Honeychurch, following his message gently correcting the errors in their family lore about Alice's having died in childbirth and poor Charles' having only originally come to America to seek work before returning to England to find that his children had been whisked away.

As much as Morton wanted to wander around the building, taking it all in, he needed to focus. Thus, he walked over to the elevators and rode to the third floor, which was dedicated to United States and Canadian research.

'Gosh!' he muttered upon seeing row after row of computer workstations, each with their own two or three monitors. He could live here quite happily ever after, he decided. It was little wonder that Maddie had elected to set up her office a mere few blocks from this treasure trove.

The room was a busy hive of quiet activity, predominantly with people wearing RootsTech lanyards, but he was able to find a vacant workstation with three computer screens. Placing his bags under the table, he logged in to his FamilySearch account, excited to be doing so for the first time in person. He used the Research Wiki to navigate to Clark County, Nevada, where Las Vegas was the county seat. Clicking *Nevada County Marriages, 1862-1993*, Morton was taken to a new search page and was relieved to see that the records included those for Clark County. However, when he checked the precise coverage, he discovered that full marriage certificates were only available from 1928 to 1954 and that a separate index ran from 1909.

He entered the name of Charles Hughes into the search box, receiving 89 results. Morton scanned down the entire list, cross-checking with the name of the spouse but finding nobody named Louise. He edited the search, amending the name to Roy Stewart but still found no Louise among the 104 results.

Morton reflected a moment, then deleted Roy's name, replacing it with Louise's in its stead, and hit the search button. Twelve results appeared, but only the top one was for someone with the fully correct name.

Louise Bullington, bride. Marriage 21 July 1923. Clark, Nevada, US. Spouse George P. Brown

Morton looked at the original entry, but it gave no additional information; it was simply an index to a marriage certificate that was not online. He gazed absent-mindedly across the active room, allowing his thoughts to process this potential development. Could George P. Brown possibly be a further pseudonym for Charles Hughes before he became Roy Stewart? If so, for how long had he been using it?

Morton ran a search for George P. Brown on the 1920 US Census. With such a common name, he also added Las Vegas to the search parameters.

He ran his eyes down the results list, pausing at the seventh entry.

Name: George Brown
Home in 1920: Las Vegas, Clark, Nevada
Birth Year: abt 1890
Birthplace: England
Relation to Head of House: Boarder

Morton viewed the full image, finding George Brown halfway down the page, living in a house on Fremont Street as a boarder in the home of Warren and Nellie Lester. He scanned across the page, taking in the full information pertaining to George.

Name: Brown, George
Relation: Boarder
Sex: Male
Race: White
Age: 30
Marital Status: Single
Can Read: Yes
Can Write: Yes
Birthplace: England
Birthplace of Father: England
Birthplace of Mother: England
Occupation: Ticket Agent
Industry: Railroad

There was absolutely nothing in the entry that proved that George Brown was another incarnation of Charles Hughes. The age, race, birthplace and the birthplaces of both parents were correct, but the name and marital status were incorrect, and the occupation bore no connection with that which Morton knew about the jobs held by Charles Hughes or Roy Stewart.

With a protracted sigh, he looked at the other entries on the page, finding that the majority of people had not been native to Nevada and that most of the men in neighbouring buildings had held employment connected to the railroad.

Running a quick Google search, he found that Las Vegas had effectively been born in 1905, when the state senator bought a ranch from the Stewart family, making it a stop-over point on the Los Angeles to Salt Lake Railroad.

Next, Morton searched for Fremont Street, finding that it still existed today but that in 1920 it had been home to the first permanent railroad station in Las Vegas. It was also right in the centre of the notorious Block 16, where gambling, prostitution and the sale of alcohol had been permitted. Going by what

Charles Hughes had confessed in his letter to his first wife, Alice, he would have been in his absolute element living on Fremont Street in 1920. But was this George Brown even him? One thing of which he needed to remind himself: Edie Loveless *was* somehow related to Juliette via Charles Hughes. The 200 centimorgans of shared DNA pointed to the correct relationship of half-first cousins once removed. Still, Morton needed more evidence.

He returned to Juliette's DNA matches on MyHeritage and checked to see whether Edie Loveless had included any form of a family tree. She had not. He weighed the time that it would take to build out her family tree from scratch against the number of hours remaining before he had to leave and instead opted to try for a simpler route.

Returning to the vital records index at FamilySearch, Morton explored the *Nevada Birth and Death Records, 1871-1992* for children born to George Brown and Louise Bullington, but was disappointed to see that among the exclusions in the dataset was Clark County. Even so, he ran a search to be certain, receiving the expected zero results.

Given the DNA confirmation, Morton decided to pursue the investigation under the working assumption that George Brown was indeed another name of Charles Hughes's. But he knew that generic searches in the major genealogy websites for a person named George Brown were far too unwieldy and onerous for the amount of time that he had left to spare.

Opening Newspapers.com, Morton tried to search for George Brown in Las Vegas for the specific period of the negative space—1918 to 1929—but there was not a single newspaper digitised for the city during this time period, and searches for the state of Nevada yielded results in the hundreds of thousands.

'Great,' Morton muttered, switching to the GenealogyBank website and attempting the same search there. He was in luck. The *Las Vegas Age* and *Las Vegas Review* had been digitised for the period in question. Now he had simply to hope that George Brown had done something newsworthy during his time in the city.

Seventy-nine results. Manageable, Morton thought, editing the display to show them in chronological order. He could see instantly from the thumbnails offered against the top two that they were incorrect, finding the words George and Brown on the same page but not in the same article.

He scrolled down, pausing at the first story which had the Christian and surnames linked together in the same sentence and was dated November 4, 1919, even though the article seemed to be pertaining to Los Angeles. The headline alone intrigued him, regardless of its possible connection to the case.

GUNMAN AT LARGE
Los Angeles, CA-
George Brown, an itinerant, who was arrested Sunday after the shooting of two in Santa Anita Canyon escaped from Monrovia jail yesterday. Officers say there is little chance of capturing the man.

Despite there being no evidence in the story, he couldn't not investigate it further. As Morton saved the article to his folder, he hoped to goodness that he wasn't about to go on a wild goose chase, wasting precious hours, albeit in genealogical heaven.

Returning to the search results, Morton could see that the next article was dated 1921 with another captivating headline, *BOOTLEGGER OPEN SEASON*, and this time it was from Las Vegas. He would return to that story but first he wanted more information on the Santa Anita Canyon shooting and to see whether he could prove that this George Brown was the same man who had married Louise Bullington.

Morton switched back to Newspapers.com and entered in the very specific dates, names and locations of the story that he wanted to read. Just one suggestion was offered from the

Monrovia Daily News.

GUNMAN STILL AT LARGE; SMALL CHANCE OF CAPTURE
Man who wounded two in Santa Anita Canyon breaks jail while awaiting trial

George Brown, an itinerant, broke free from jail yesterday afternoon following the shooting of James Summer and Sylvia McAloon in Santa Anita Canyon.
Brown spent Sunday night in the Monrovia jail and was awaiting arraignment yesterday in Judge Burr's court.
Out of consideration for the man's comfort, a constable allowed Brown the freedom of the entire room, rather than confine him to the steel cell. Sometime between noon and one o'clock Brown picked the lock on the rear door of the jail and slipped away. He has not been seen since.
There is about one chance in six of capturing the man, according to the officers here. It is understood that Summer, who was shot in the head by a stray bullet from Brown's automatic, is in a serious condition at a Pasadena hospital. McAloon was not seriously injured.

Morton couldn't help but sigh. Another story with no evidence linking the man to Charles Hughes. He downloaded the article, then brought forward the dates of his search to try and find a story that covered the actual shooting. He found it in the previous day's edition of the same newspaper.

GUN PLAY AND HARD LIQUOR
Man is shot through eye, Girl in back, innocent victims of mountain quarrel

George Brown, held in this city for the alleged shooting of his companions yesterday in Santa Anita Canyon, escaped from the jail by picking the lock early this afternoon. Police are now making a thorough search for the prisoner.

Too much hard liquor is given as the main reason why George Brown, 29, of no fixed abode, shot and injured James Summer and Sylvia McAloon yesterday afternoon during a riotous fight six miles above the mount of Big Santa Anita Canyon. Brown is now in the Monrovia jail.

Summer and McAloon were hit by the same bullet. The ball pierced the walls of a dance hall, struck Summer in the eye, coming out of the head in front of the ear and cutting open the ear. It then hit Miss McAloon in the back, inflicting a flesh wound, went through the walls of the dance hall and ripped a hole in the hat-brim of a third bystander on the outside. Neither Summer nor Miss McAloon were taking part in any fight.

The affair, according to accounts given to Constable Quiggle and Forest Ranger A.J. Mueller, started when Brown accused Los Angeles man, Fred Phillips of being a host to evil spirits. Brown is alleged to have taken his gun, a 25-caliber Colt automatic, from his inner coat pocket and transferred it to his hip pocket as he approached Phillips. Witnesses quote Brown as being very drunk and shouting obscenities at Phillips, accusing him of devilry and witchcraft. Brown shot twice, one bullet going wild and the other entering the dance hall and wounding Summer and the girl.

Immediately following the shooting the crowd overpowered Brown and roughly manhandled him. Threats of lynching the man were heard on all sides when Ranger Mueller arrived on the scene.

Miss McAloon was able to ride a horse down the trail and is believed not seriously injured. Summer is expected to lose the sight of his eye and was unable to walk or ride out of the canyon.

Morton stared at the article. If the correct age of the man and the mention of devilry and witchcraft hadn't been enough to persuade Morton that George Brown was Charles Hughes, then the photograph featured below the story and captioned as *George Brown* certainly was. A grainy, black-and-white image— possibly an early police mugshot—showed the face of a man staring blankly at the camera. Despite the lack of clarity, the image was unmistakably that of Charles Hughes.

Chapter Ten

4th March 2023, Salt Lake City, Utah, USA

The negative space in Charles Hughes's life had just decreased. Morton had added a second *Also Known As* to his profile and also saved the newspaper article, the 1920 Census entry and the marriage to Louise Bullington.

'Well, you certainly kept all that quiet when you were busy confessing your sins,' Morton said to Charles Hughes's profile picture. 'Just you wait until Margot hears about what you've been up to.'

With the new information saved, Morton had run an immigration search under the name of George Brown, but there were too many possibilities to be certain. Whenever and wherever the man had arrived in the United States, he had certainly been in Los Angeles, California by November 1919. There, he had absconded from jail and, by the time of the 1920 Census, he had been living in Las Vegas. His marriage to Louise Bullington in July 1923 now marked the commencement of the revised negative space, ending in January 1929 with his third marriage to Beulah Hennes.

The final dots were joining together in Charles Hughes's life; Morton hoped that, by returning to his original newspaper search at GenealogyBank, he might just be able to add some information to those undiscovered six years.

The subsequent article to the one that had sent him off on a tangent was dated March 22, 1921, and came from the *Las Vegas Age* newspaper. Morton clicked to read the full story.

BOOTLEGGER OPEN SEASON
The advent of the prohibition agents' raid in Las Vegas has evidently made the city officers wake up and take notice, and the 'still' season has now been

declared open, until such time as it is deemed advisable to cease hunting. On Saturday night, in the neighborhood of 7 or 8 o'clock, the officers captured a twenty-gallon still and attachments in the home of Mr George Brown. The defendant, owner of a notorious speakeasy on Fremont Street was arrested and the still locked up for safe keeping in the county jail. The still was found with eight gallons of finished product on hand along with substantial quantities of prune and apricot mash which was getting in shape for further operation. Bail was furnished on Tuesday and Mr Brown, having heard the complaint read, pleaded guilty, and on Wednesday was in court for sentence. The judge imposed a $600 fine, which the defendant duly paid.

Owner of a notorious speakeasy on Fremont Street? Morton read again with a smile. Charles Hughes was certainly an ancestor whose backstory just kept on giving. On top of his many misdemeanours, Morton could now add bootlegging during the prohibition era to the list.

He saved the story, Morton then moved on chronologically, reading another story, dated April 4, 1922.

SEIZE LARGE STILL AND NAB FOUR MEN IN LAS VEGAS RAID
Four men were arrested, and a fifty-gallon still with a quantity of liquor were seized in a raid on a farm near Las Vegas from which prohibition agents returned last night. The men are said to have engaged in liquor manufacture to sell in large quantities in various Block 16 speakeasies. Fifty gallons of corn whisky and 350 gallons of mash were found on the premises owned by George Brown of Fremont Street. The four men were placed under a bond of $2,000 each, which they duly settled.

He read the story three times, slightly amazed by what he was learning, although nothing Charles Hughes did should surprise him anymore.

The first thing that struck Morton as noteworthy was the sheer escalation in illegal liquor production in just a single year.

Evidently, the man's reaction to arrest and having his still confiscated had been to invest in a much larger-scale enterprise outside of the city itself, where he had presumably hoped that he would be left to his own illegal devices. What an absolute change in fortunes for a man described as itinerant just two years prior. Now, here he had shown up, easily paying a bond of $2,000 to leave jail.

As Morton saved the story to Charles Hughes's profile, he wondered about the man's state of mind. Evidently, he had stopped running away from his demons and had embraced them wholeheartedly in his life in prohibition-era Las Vegas.

Morton yawned and gazed around the room, realising that he was hungry and thirsty. He probably should visit the break room on the ground floor and get something to eat and drink. He had overheard someone at RootsTech talking about a fun rocking chair there and vending machines with ice cream. But then he noticed the time; he had just over an hour until he would have to leave for the airport.

Morton looked around himself incredulously, as though he might spy the culprit who had stolen the past few hours from him. Now what? The searches that he was currently running he could literally do anywhere in the world with a Wi-Fi signal. He was sitting in the largest genealogical library in the world but— beyond the luxury of three screens—was not making any use of it. Food, drink and newspaper searches into Charles Hughes's bootlegging days would have to wait while he prioritised research that could only be carried out within this very building.

Opening up the FamilySearch website, Morton clicked on *Search FamilySearch Library Catalog* and entered *Las Vegas* into the box. There were over one thousand books in the building that fulfilled the search criteria. Several on the first pages alone caught his attention: *Las Vegas: as it began, as it grew*; *The Prospector (Las Vegas)*; *The First 100: portraits of the men and women who shaped Las Vegas*; *Tales of Las Vegas*; *Early Las Vegas...* Among these relevant titles were also genealogies of Las Vegas families, church histories, newspaper clippings and indexes to various records. He literally could spend days here just on this single aspect of the case.

Most of the books were found on shelves on the third floor, where he was currently researching. He turned to the lady working to his left, and said, 'Sorry, would you mind keeping an eye on my stuff while I go and get some books?'

The lady smiled. 'Sure. But this is probably about the safest place in the world. I think your stuff is good.'

Morton thanked her, wrote the shelf number 979.3 on his hand, and headed off in search of the books. He quickly found the correct location but was daunted by the sheer amount that could be relevant. He wasn't sure if there was a limit to the number of books that he could take back to his desk, but he slid out five that seemed to him most likely to be of use and returned to his desk.

'I had to fight them all off,' the lady beside him said as he sat down at his desk.

'Pardon?' Morton questioned.

'All those bad guys that were lining up to take all your stuff,' she quipped.

Morton grinned. 'Thank you.'

'You're so welcome,' she replied with a smile.

With a defeatist sigh, Morton opened the first book. 'Here we go,' he muttered quietly as he began scanning through the first pages at a speed with which he was uncomfortable. He much preferred taking his time, digesting the information, making notes and conducting further tangential research as he went. But this was different; this was skim-reading and making hasty scribbles to be followed up at a later time.

He found the early history of Las Vegas fascinating in and of itself. He loved the tales of the early pioneers settling the Wild West. Knowing that Juliette's great-grandfather was out here, among the infamous bootleggers, made it all the more interesting. Perhaps when the kids were a bit older, they could come out here as a family and retrace Charles Hughes's journey from sleepy Etchingham through Los Angeles and prohibition-era Las Vegas, and on to Prescott, Arizona.

As he progressed through the various books, so Morton's knowledge of the place and period grew. He learnt that prohibition in Las Vegas had only been half-heartedly enforced, being somewhat protected by the city's isolation in the Nevada desert. The state legislature had also voted to repeal prohibition in 1923, meaning that speakeasies had become able to operate openly with only occasional raids taking place by police from Los Angeles or San Francisco.

Morton photographed a page from one book, which talked about the Block 16 speakeasies being the beating heart of the roaring 1920s, providing illegal liquor, cultivated jazz music and a place in which flappers could exist on an equal footing to the men; men who otherwise would have mainly frequented the traditional saloons without women.

He read about one of the biggest prohibition raids in Las Vegas, which took place in 1928 when the feds stormed all the major speakeasies of the time: the Arizona Club, Green Lantern, Honolulu Inn, Pastime, Big Four, Brookside, Miners Club and Jazz Bar.

Morton re-read the names of the speakeasies. *Brookside?* Hadn't that been the name of the family home in Etchingham that Charles had fled from? He quickly checked his profile and found that it had been. Coincidence? One of the newspaper articles, which he had read, certainly said that George Brown had been an owner of a Block 16 speakeasy. Was it just circumstantial evidence or had he named his speakeasy after his abandoned former home in England?

Even though he had just ten minutes left until he had to leave, and still had another tome to flick through, Morton slid the books to one side and ran a search in GenealogyBank for *Brookside* and *Block 16* in Las Vegas during the 1920s. He clicked to read the first of several articles.

WOMEN PEDDLE BOOZE

It is not generally known that women are becoming in some instances the most vicious violators of our prohibition laws. Yesterday afternoon pleas of guilty to possession charges were made by two women before Justice of the Peace Frank Davis. The two women, Grace Williams and Louise Bullington were fined $250 each or given the alternative of 125 days in the county jail. They were arrested in a raid at the speakeasy, "Brookside" in Block 16, along with four other individuals connected to bootlegging.

'They are carrying liquor in containers under their waist,' the Chief of Police had said, showing in court a copper tank, constructed like a baseball catcher's chest protector.

The two women are both in the county jail in lieu of sufficient funds to pay the fines.

'Wow,' Morton said, and not for the first time while working on this case. He scrolled up to see the date of the article: 6th February 1923. Five months before George Brown would go on to marry Louise Bullington. Was she working for him as a bootlegger and then ended up marrying him? What had happened to make him once again abandon this wife to start a new life in Arizona with a third spouse anew?

Morton's phone vibrated in his pocket. It was his alarm telling him that it was time to leave. Sure enough, genealogy had once again warped time.

While he had his mobile in his hand, he checked his emails and found that he had a reply waiting for him on MyHeritage from Edie Loveless.

Hi Morton

I'd be very happy to meet you tomorrow. I suggest we meet outside the Mob Museum at 10 am. Make sure you have at least a couple of hours free!

Edie

Mob Museum? Only Las Vegas would have one of those, Morton reasoned. He quickly Googled its location, finding that it was on Stewart Avenue, right in the centre of the former Block 16. As he packed up his things, he had an ominous feeling about what he was going to find out.

Morton tried to take in as much of the library as he could, feeling as though he was leaving the party too soon. With two bags full of DNA kits and a head full of stories about Juliette's great-grandfather, Morton left the building with a confident swagger.

His walk said it all.

Chapter Eleven

5th March 2023, Las Vegas, Nevada, USA

Like most buildings in Las Vegas, the Mob Museum was huge; but unlike most buildings in Las Vegas, it appeared to have some history to it. Morton was standing at the foot of the wide flight of steps that led up to the five-storey neoclassical museum. He had arrived early and was unable to resist sticking his head inside and asking the security guard on duty if the place really was as old as it was being portrayed, or if it was actually little more than a garish replica; like the Eiffel Tower or the Statue of Liberty which he had seen.

'It's as historic as it comes in Vegas,' the guard had said with a chuckle. 'Built in the 1930s as a post office and the city courthouse. All kinds of important stuff happened in here before it became a museum. The Kefauver Committee hearings took place right here in the 1950s, don't you know?'

'Oh, wow,' Morton had replied, not having ever heard of the Kefauver Committee hearings but not wishing to look ignorant or to offend. 'I'll try and squeeze in a visit before I leave.'

'You do that,' the guard answered.

He stepped back outside and promptly Googled the Kefauver Committee hearings, thereby discovering that they had been held in 1950 by the US Senate Special Committee to investigate organised crime in interstate commerce and successfully exposed much of the underbelly of organised crime across America.

Morton was staring up at the solid blue skies behind the museum when he sensed someone approaching him.

'Morton Farrier?'

'Yes!' he answered the exotic-looking lady standing close by.

She was in her late seventies or early eighties, with bright purple spring-like hair, lime-green glasses perched on the end of her nose and a flowing silk pashmina covered in orange skulls. Both arms were adorned with an eclectic variety of bangles. Very Las Vegas, he thought.

He offered her his hand to shake, but she leant in and kissed him on both cheeks. 'My half-first cousin...once removed...in-law!' she declared wildly.

Morton grinned. 'Lovely to meet you. It's such a shame my wife couldn't be here to meet you, too. She'd love all this. Especially since she's a police officer.'

Edie's eyes widened and she pushed her glasses back onto the bridge of her nose. 'Gosh. And tell me, does she know all that her great-grandfather got up to?'

Morton shook his head and said, 'I'm not sure *I* know all that he got up to yet.'

'Well, it sure is your lucky day because you're about to find out,' Edie said with a laugh. 'Shall we go in?'

'Oh, we're going *inside?*' he questioned, now unsure why this should have come as a surprise to him, since it had been their agreed rendezvous point.

'Hell, yeah,' Edie cried, linking her arm through his and walking up the steps into the building. Morton purchased tickets for the two of them at one of the booths just inside the main entrance, slightly perplexed.

'Let's head downstairs to the speakeasy first,' Edie suggested, guiding him towards the elevators. 'I could sure use a cocktail and you're *absolutely* gonna need one. That's if you have the time?'

'Oh, I've got a couple of hours until I need to head off to the airport,' Morton said.

'That's perfect, we should be able to cover it all in that time.'

In light of his recent discoveries, he delighted in being able to experience the museum's basement speakeasy. No windows, bare brick and muted lighting gave it the atmospheric edge of the period. The space was occupied by an assortment of circular tables and chairs, situated around various exhibits relating to the prohibition era.

Edie led them over to the L-shaped wooden bar, hopping up onto a barstool at one corner, as though she were a regular here. Morton half-expected her to shout over to the barman by name and say that she wanted her usual.

'Good afternoon, guys,' the barman said, handing them a thin black menu each.

Without opening the menu, she turned to Morton, took off her glasses and pointed at him. 'You like coffee?'

'Do I like coffee? I practically live on coffee,' he answered.

Edie waved her hands excitedly, then put her glasses back on. 'You have to get the Last Night In Vegas,' she instructed, opening his menu for him and pointing it out. She knew exactly where it was and what it was.

'*Bourbon, fernet menta and cold brew coffee,*' he read. 'Sounds good. And it fits; it *is* my last night in Vegas.'

Edie laughed. 'Well, what do you know? But I think it's more *last night* in Vegas. You know what I mean? Rather than last night in Vegas.'

Morton blushed at his stupidity.

'Two *Last Night* in Vegases, please, sir,' Edie ordered, pointing again. 'And don't you go sparing on the bourbon.'

'Sure,' he replied. 'Anything to eat?'

Edie looked at him. 'Are you hungry? I can always eat a little something. The hummus plate is good to share.'

'Sounds perfect,' Morton replied. 'I reckon my next meal will be on the flight at about eleven o'clock tonight.'

'Oh, well, you should eat something, then,' she said, placing down her menu. She placed her hand on Morton's arm. 'I'm just so happy to meet up with another relative. I'll tell you… It was matching up on MyHeritage with a lady called Bernadette Honeychurch, and exchanging emails with her, that I found out more about my grandfather, or Roy Stewart, that is, as you and

Bernadette knew him.'

Morton grinned. 'Actually… He went by the name of Charles Hughes when he lived in England.'

Edie's eyes widened impressively. 'What? Bernadette never told me this!'

'Well, she didn't know.'

'Boy, it looks like we have *a lot* to tell each other,' Edie said, just as the barman placed two cocktail glasses down onto black serviettes in front of them.

'Enjoy,' he said, taking a retreating bow.

'It looks really good,' Morton observed, picking up the dark drink with a white frothy top. 'Cheers.'

'Cheers to my new favourite relatives!' Edie said, tapping her glass against his. She slumped back on the barstool with a groan of pleasure. She moved in closer to him and lowered her voice. 'Sometimes I use my Nevada resident discount to get in here half-price and just come for the cocktails. I guess I take after my rogue of a grandfather on that one.'

Morton laughed. 'I think my wife's love of wine might have come from him, too.'

'So, come on. You're telling me that my grandfather lived in England under a different name?' she asked, dramatically throwing her hands in the air.

'Uh-huh,' he answered, taking a sip of the cocktail before beginning to relay all that he knew about Charles Hughes's early life. When he spoke about the family home of Brookside in Etchingham, Edie confirmed that that was the exact name that he had given to his Block 16 speakeasy. It was at that point that Edie fished a small, tatty, rectangular piece of orange card from the bag on her shoulder. In bold capital letters in the centre was the word *BROOKSIDE*. Below it was written *Fremont Street, Las Vegas. For Unadulterated Liquors.*

'It was a membership card for the speakeasy. They didn't have too much bother from the agents in Vegas, but, you see, this was another way of making sure there were no undercover agents trying to muscle in and shut the place down.'

'Mind if I take a photo, so that I can show it to Juliette?' Morton asked.

'You go right ahead. Is it really light enough in here to get a good shot?'

'It should be okay,' Morton answered, taking a picture on his mobile phone regardless. He was tempted to send it to Juliette with no explanation but decided to wait for a big reveal with Margot, instead.

As Morton explained about Charles Hughes's war service in the Royal Engineers and his belief that Charles had likely suffered from PTSD, the waiter placed a plate of food between them. In the centre was a blob of hummus and around it were arranged a selection of olives, carrot sticks and toasted pitta.

'Well, it's funny you should say that,' Edie said. 'My great-aunt said that he spent some time in an asylum because of the voices he was hearing, but I've never found any evidence and I think she might have just been trying to poison my mother against him. Sorry, I'm interrupting... Carry on with your story.'

'That's almost it, really. Then he just...upped and left one day, leaving a note on the table for his wife, Alice,' Morton concluded, popping an olive into his mouth. 'Nothing was heard from him until 1939, when he wrote a letter of confession to Alice and his two kids back in England. He seemed to have forgotten about his second wife and child, though, in his confession of wicked deeds. And that's the end of part one.'

'Hmm. The death of Charles Hughes,' Edie commented, 'before the birth of George Brown.'

'Exactly.'

Edie took a big drink of the cocktail, then said, 'George's life was pretty eventful, and it would take *a lot* of cocktails to tell you everything. Tonight would most certainly *not* be your last night in Vegas. Why don't you tell me what you know already about his time as George, and I'll fill in the gaps—at least, the ones that I know about.'

Morton told her everything that he had discovered but with the caveat that he was only part-way through his newspaper search into George Brown's life in Las Vegas. He told Edie that he had found mention of her grandmother, Louise Bullington, in the newspapers and had found a reference to their marriage but not the actual certificate.

'Now, I got something else in here that might help,' Edie muttered, rummaging about again in her shoulder bag. She handed Morton a small, folded document that was obviously old and well-handled. He carefully opened it out to find that it was an original marriage certificate between George Brown and Louise Bullington.

'That's so funny,' Morton said, observing that the groom's parents were noted as Edward Brown and Caroline Longley. 'Apart from his father's surname, he actually gave the correct names of his parents.'

'I guess lies based on the truth must have come easier to tell,' Edie said, finishing her cocktail. She clapped her hands together, jiggling the bangles on her wrists. 'So, as you correctly assumed, my grandparents met at the Brookside speakeasy on Fremont Street. She came from a bit of a rough background and got a job there, bootlegging. You see, it was generally frowned upon to stop and search women at the time, so they obviously made the best bootleggers.'

'Oh, I see,' Morton said. 'And then they fell in love and the rest, as they say, is history.'

Edie laughed. 'Well, that's a romantic way of looking at their story.'

'But not the truth?'

Edie shrugged. She dipped a piece of pitta into the hummus and ate it. 'I'll let you be the judge. Finish your drink and we'll head upstairs.'

Morton was surprised that Edie's part of the story had ended so suddenly. He dutifully did as instructed and finished his cocktail.

'Come on, the top floor awaits us,' she said, linking arms with him and walking back towards the lift. As they headed up, she asked him, 'So, you weren't here on vacation, then? Was it business that took you to Salt Lake?'

'Kind of. I was speaking at a genealogy conference. That's my job, you see. I'm a genealogist.'

Edie looked at him with her mouth open. 'That explains a lot. I was thinking it was a little weird how informed and involved you were in your wife's great-grandfather's life.'

'To be honest with you, it's really always been more of an addiction than a job for me,' he explained with a smile.

'I can imagine,' she agreed, stepping out of the lift. 'Now, this floor—in fact, this whole building—is so fascinating that you'll need to spend hours here but, in the interests of part two of his life, we're just going to head straight on through to a certain place.'

Edie led them past exhibits on the Mob and organised crime into a room with plush, red, patterned wallpaper and glass cabinets full of artefacts related to the early days of Las Vegas. Judging by the pull on his arm, she was taking him to a series of framed photographs on one wall. She stood back and studied him. 'You see it?'

Morton took a quick glance at the series of images that appeared to show an evolution in the nascent days of Block 16. He scanned the captions until he spotted a street scene with the caption, *Fremont Street, 1921*. He guessed that this was the one in which he should be seeing something. The black-and-white picture was taken low to the ground in the middle of a wide street which was lined with shops and businesses. A contemporary car was parked on the left and behind it were two horses pulling a cart. The pavements were busy with people, but if he was expected to see Charles Hughes among them, he couldn't, as their faces were not identifiable. 'Is it this one?' he questioned Edie.

She nodded enthusiastically.

He took a step closer and began scrutinising the image further, bringing back his training from Dr Baumgartner in photo forensics. In the foreground on the left was a vertical sign for the Las Vegas Hotel and beside that was a restaurant and bakery. Immediately in the centre at the rear of the picture was a building that looked like the railway station. Morton moved his gaze to the buildings on the right of the street and finally spotted it: a sign with *Brookside* running vertically down a squat, two-storey building with a first-floor balcony.

'Brookside,' Morton said with a smile.

'That was the very speakeasy where it all happened,' Edie declared.

Morton took out his mobile phone and took a photograph of it to add to Charles Hughes's profile.

'And, right outside the building—just about where that horse and cart are, I'd say—was where my grandfather, George, shot and killed someone.'

'Oh, dear,' Morton said. 'Hounded by the devil again?'

'You could call her that. Or you could call her Louise.'

'Louise?' Morton repeated, staring at Edie. 'As in Louise-Bullington Louise—?'

'Uh-huh.'

Chapter Twelve

5th March 2023, Las Vegas, Nevada, USA

'Any reason?' Morton asked. 'Or was it like most things Charles did that defied explanation?'

Edie took hold of his arm. 'Let's keep going.'

'Oh, God. I don't like the sound of that,' Morton said, making Edie laugh as she guided them into the next room of exhibits. They walked past a bullet-ridden, solid brick wall behind a protective glass screen. Etched onto the glass in a white, art deco font was written, *St Valentine's Day Massacre Wall*.

'Is that the *actual* wall?' Morton asked.

'Sure is,' Edie answered. 'It was taken down brick by brick and erected in a nightclub in Vancouver before finding its way here.'

They walked on a little further and then stopped beside a display, entitled ENFORCING PROHIBITION. Below the photographs of various people adorning the wall were white captions on red boxes. Morton glanced over each of the names: *Daisy Simpson, Lady Hooch Hunter; Mabel Willebrandt, First Lady of the Law; Eugene Jackson, killed in the Line of Duty; Izzy and Moe, Agents in Disguise* and, finally, *Louise Bullington, Bootlegger or Agent?*

The photograph of Louise was actually in some kind of a document resembling a folded-open passport. On the top half were two close-up pictures of Louise—looking forwards and in profile—embossed with an official stamp that Morton was unable to read. On the lower half, the words THE UNITED STATES arced over TREASURY DEPARTMENT and INTERNAL REVENUE SERVICE. Morton read on. *This certifies that Louise Bullington of Las Vegas is duly employed as a Federal Prohibition Agent and is hereby authorized to execute and perform all the duties delegated to such officers by law.*

'She was an agent?' Morton said, clearly aghast.

'Uh-huh,' Edie confirmed. 'And notice anything else about her ID card?'

'Is that...? Is that what I think it is?' Morton asked, seeing what appeared to be blood spatter across the top of the document.

'Yeah. Read the caption and it'll tell you all about it.'

Morton took a breath and read.

Louise Bullington, one of just a dozen women who served as prohibition agents, worked undercover in Las Vegas. But was she working as a bootlegger, a government agent or both? Louise was herself arrested in February 1923 for bootlegging for a man named George Brown, who ran a speakeasy on Fremont Street, yet her agent's identity card (above) shows the date September 6, 1922. Despite the obvious conflict, Louise and George married in July 1923. It is unknown if Louise maintained her role as a prohibition agent after they married, but in 1925, when the government banned female agents, Louise's husband, George discovered her secret. In a dramatic showdown outside his speakeasy, George shot and killed Louise then fled the city, leaving their two-year-old daughter an orphan. According to local reports at the time, Louise was clutching her identity card as she died.

'Your mum was the two-year-old orphan?' Morton questioned.

'Yeah, that's right.'

'Did she remember them at all?' Morton asked. 'Her parents, I mean?'

Edie shook her head. 'No. No memory at all. She was raised by an aunt who told her nothing at all about her father but kept her mother's memory alive as best she could. Mom found out a few things as she got older, mainly that her father was a bootlegging scoundrel, but nothing about where he came from or where he went. I found out a lot from doing research on the ground—newspaper searches, that kind of thing—about his life here in Vegas, but it wasn't until I took the MyHeritage DNA test that I linked up with Bernadette Honeychurch and she told me exactly what happened to George Brown: he changed into Roy Stewart!' Edie shook her head. 'You just couldn't make it up.'

'And there you have it: the three lives of Charles Hughes,' Morton concluded.

'Yeah.' Edie turned to him and asked, 'Have you got time, before you leave, for me to show you where Brookside was?'

Morton looked at his watch. 'I've got about forty-five minutes and counting but I'd really love to see it.'

'Let's go,' she said, leading the way with purpose. Gesturing to the exhibits around them, she added, 'You'll just have to come on back with Juliette to see the rest of this. It'll blow your mind.'

'Oh, she would love it,' he replied, catching fleeting glances of the display cabinets containing weapons, coroner records and the original bullets that killed those in the St Valentine's Day Massacre in 1929. Maybe Juliette wouldn't love it after all.

They found themselves back at the elevator, riding down to the ground floor. They walked out into the warmth of the afternoon sunshine and down the flight of steps to the pavement.

Edie led them one block south to East Ogden Avenue, where she stopped and said, 'So, right now, you're standing in the centre of what was Block 16—the original Vegas.'

Morton looked around. Nothing whatsoever resembled the historic photographs displayed inside the museum. He recalled the Bubba Gump Shrimp Company's waitress saying that if something's old in Vegas, it gets torn down or blown up.

'Can you imagine what Charles George Roy would have made of this place now?' Edie asked. 'Gambling, liquor and women—all he seemed to live for.'

Morton smiled as they walked another block south and then

one block west. 'Wow,' he muttered. Fremont street had been pedestrianised with a canopy that curved down over the entire street for as far as he could see in either direction.

'Welcome to the Fremont Street Experience,' Edie said. 'Twelve million LED lights and a 550,000-watt sound system. Recognise it?'

Morton looked at her, slightly bewildered, then up and down the busy street. Everything was glitzy, flashing and modern. There was literally nothing at all that he recognised. 'Nope,' he finally concluded.

'Get that picture up that you took inside the museum of Fremont Street in 1921.'

Morton again did as instructed and held his phone's screen towards her.

Edie looked at the image, then moved his arm so that the old photograph was framed between the two rows of buildings.

'Is that *here?*' Morton asked, unable to find any resemblance at all. The only thing similar was the width of the street. Switching his focus between the two images—roughly one hundred years apart—he tried to see where the speakeasy had been located.

'Brookside was a little further down,' Edie said, intuiting his thoughts.

They continued on through the throng of people moving in and out of the casinos and gift shops that dominated the street, until Edie brought them to a stop and pointed at a building. 'It was right about here.'

'The Las Vegas Club,' Morton said, reading the neon letters on the front and side of the building. All the windows and doors were covered with photos of women in low-cut, black tops, smiling as they held out a hand of playing cards. According to the quote on the door, it was *the ultimate Las Vegas party spot*. 'I have to say… I think Charles would be very proud.'

'George would be even prouder,' Edie quipped.

'But Roy might have disapproved,' Morton added, frowning,

110

and made Edie laugh.

They stood in silence for a moment, with Morton trying to reconcile all that he had learned about Juliette's great-grandfather. Even though he felt as though the last few days had been a whistle-stop tour, this was a meaningful location at which to end his trip. 'Thank you so much for taking the time to meet me and show me around,' he said to Edie. 'It's been such a pleasure.'

'I'm *so* delighted that you got in touch with me, Morton,' she said. 'It's been so wonderful to share all this with you. I feel like between us we've got a much fuller picture of my grandfather, now.'

'The deserter's tale in three acts,' Morton said.

'It's been wonderful. But too brief. I want you to come back with your wife and kids.'

'So do I. You know, you're also very welcome to come and stay with us in Rye, if ever you're in the neighbourhood,' Morton replied.

Edie winked. 'I might just take you up on that offer and you can show me the other version of Brookside.'

Morton laughed. 'It's *slightly* less glitzy and glamorous than this. I'm just saying…'

Edie shrugged. 'It's obviously still an important part of the family history.'

'Yes, it is,' he agreed, glancing at his watch and seeing that it was time to leave.

'Well, I know you need to get your flight. So, you take care,' Edie said, pulling him into a full embrace.

'And you,' Morton replied. 'Listen, can I get you an Uber somewhere?'

Edie waved her hands dismissively. 'I might just head back to the Mob Museum for another cocktail.'

'Well, you enjoy it. And do have another for me,' he said. He repeated his goodbyes and watched her saunter back in the direction from which they had come.

Morton couldn't help but smile as he stared absent-mindedly at the Las Vegas Club, thinking of Edie, Charles Hughes's complicated story, his trip to Salt Lake City, his talks, seeing Maddie again and the idea of being reunited with his family tomorrow.

'Pretty hot, huh?' someone said out of nowhere.

Morton looked at a heavily bearded, overweight man with one arm missing and a US flag draped over his shoulders. 'Sorry, pardon?'

'Them women you're staring at in the photos—they're hot. They're even hotter inside,' he stated.

'Oh, I wasn't… I wasn't looking at the women—,' he started to explain.

'Hey. No judgement here, man; you're in Vegas.' The man strolled away singing to himself.

After one final glance up and down Fremont Street, it was time for Morton to go to the airport for his night flight home.

Chapter Thirteen

6th March 2023, M25 motorway, Surrey, England

Morton was driving down the M25 motorway a few miles out of Heathrow Airport. Having again flown business class with a seat that converted into a bed, he had managed to sleep most of the way home and had actually arrived feeling quite refreshed rather than exhausted as he had felt on the trip out to America.

As he drove, he mulled over the Charles Hughes case, excited to tell Juliette and Margot all about his discoveries. In the airport lounge in Las Vegas, Morton had typed up and collated all of his findings into one document from which he had hastily created a presentation to show the family this evening. He had completed his newspaper searches into George Brown's antics in Las Vegas, confirming all that he had been told by Edie Loveless.

He passed a road sign for the upcoming Brighton-bound exit to the M23 and his thoughts turned to something that Edie had said to him in the Mob Museum speakeasy: George Brown had spent time in an asylum after hearing voices in his head, but she hadn't been able to find any evidence to corroborate the fact. But what if he had entered the asylum in England under his birth name, Charles Hughes?

Morton looked at the clock: 2:12 pm. The kids were still at school and Juliette would likely still be at work. He indicated to pull off the motorway and took the M23 south towards Brighton with an idea in his head.

Forty-five minutes later, Morton parked his Mini in the carpark of The Keep—the county archive for the whole of East Sussex. He strode through the entrance door to reception. He could have sworn that he felt his soul leave his body when he saw that behind the desk was Miss Deidre Latimer. Almost every archive that Morton visited had an officious, unhelpful and miserable archivist, but none of them compared to the woman standing in front of him with her arms folded across her chest. She was definitely the dragon guarding the entrance to The Keep.

'Oh, you're back, then?' Miss Latimer said flatly.

'Yes,' he answered, signing in. 'My recent cases haven't warranted coming here, but this latest one does.'

'No. I meant back from RootsTech,' she clarified, giving him an icy glare.

How on earth did she know that he had been to RootsTech? She would literally be the last person on the planet that he would have told.

'A friend of mine attended and saw you,' she explained.

'Oh, right,' Morton said, a realisation dawning on him. He hoped to goodness that she wasn't about to mention his talk on researching Sussex ancestors.

'Yes, she attended your talk on researching Sussex ancestors,' she said.

Morton flushed crimson. 'I… I hope she enjoyed it.'

Miss Latimer took in a long breath and raised her eyes. 'She said it was okay. She didn't learn anything she didn't already know, I think were her exact words. Rather odd that they picked *you* for it, isn't it, don't you think?'

Morton shrugged, heading off towards the lockers.

'She did mention you joking about keeping an eye out for a demon archivist,' Miss Latimer called after him.

Morton stopped in his tracks against his will, turned and offered a wooden smile. As often happened in her presence, words failed him. Give him an awkward conversation with his ex-girlfriend after a twenty-six-year absence over having to talk to Deidre Latimer any day.

'I can't for the life of me think to whom you could have been referring,' she continued, mocking deep thinking as she stared into the air. 'None of the staff here fit that description at all.'

'Maybe you've never been on the other side of the desk to her,' Morton returned, pleased with himself for his comeback.

'Hmm,' she murmured. 'No, I rather think that all of the staff here remain professional and courteous at all times. And, you know, that's in spite of the occasional customer who drops in, thinking they're the world's greatest gift to genealogy and yet who also seem entirely incapable of abiding by the simplest of archive rules, and whose fantastical and unbelievable actions and situations that they find themselves in are simply preposterous and serve only to bring the whole profession into disrepute.'

'Hmm,' Morton replied. 'I can't for the life of me think who you're referring to.'

In a fluster, Morton stowed his bag in the locker and carried his laptop, pencil and notepad into the reading room. He had no idea if the records that he wanted even existed, never mind if there was space in the Reading Room to examine them, but he was not about to extend his conversation with Miss Latimer any more than was absolutely necessary to find out.

Just inside the Reading Room, he found Quiet Brian sitting at a small desk, examining a document with a magnifying glass. 'Afternoon,' Morton greeted.

'Good afternoon,' Quiet Brian said quietly, looking up from his reading. 'How can I help you?'

'I believe that my wife's great-grandfather, who lived in Etchingham, entered an asylum at some point between 1918 and 1920,' Morton said. 'Do you have any records for that time?'

'Well, the county asylum at that point was Hellingly,' Quiet Brian explained. 'And yes, we do have records. But, for obvious reasons, there are strict closure rules. Let me take a look.' He started typing on the computer.

Morton knew Hellingly Hospital well. Back in 2011, he had been researching a suicide at the asylum in 1924. It had been whilst investigating this case that he had first met Juliette when she had been working as an assistant at Hailsham Library. He remembered with a smile their first date in The White Hart pub. When he had mentioned the case to her, she had suggested they visit the derelict asylum site and they had ended up wandering the graffitied corridors with smashed windows, collapsed ceilings and serious attempts at arson. Something that had been spray-painted on the walls suddenly came back to him: *IN A MAD WORLD, ONLY THE MAD ARE SANE*. Fun times.

'So, the original case books have been digitised,' Quiet Brian read. 'You're after HE 27/2. Now, they're available on any of those computers over there.' He pointed over at the four rows of computer terminals, only a handful of which were occupied. He noted down the reference number on a piece of scrap paper and handed it to Morton.

'Thank you,' he said, taking the paper and heading over to the nearest computer. Morton easily navigated through the ever-increasing number of digitised images to the records for East Sussex County Asylum and was thankful to find that, despite there being no index, the original ledger had been completed in alphabetical order.

As he was dipping in and out of the images, jumping his way through them towards surnames beginning with H, Morton's phone vibrated in his pocket. He took it out to see that he had a message from Juliette.

Er…what are you doing?

Accompanying the image was a screenshot of a map showing his precise location. Whoops. He had been rumbled.

It's a VERY quick bit of research for your great-grandfather on my way home. I'll be leaving in ten minutes! Can't wait to see you all xx

Juliette replied instantly with an eye-rolling emoji.
He needed to be quick.

Morton clicked on an image and found that it was for surnames beginning with G. He stopped choosing files at random and clicked through the subsequent three images until he reached H. Then, he slowly and carefully read down the list of surnames. The second to last entry on the first page was for a Charles Hughes. Morton excitedly ran his finger across the line to try and ascertain if it was the correct person.

Date of Admission: 27th December 1918
Admission Register Number: 3423
Name of Patient: Charles Hughes
To What Union Chargeable: Etchingham
Situation: Male wing. Ground Floor
Form of Mental Disorder: Mania
Age of First Attack: 28
Removed, Recovered or Dead: Absconded
Date: 19th April 1919

Not for the first time, Morton was surprised by Charles Hughes's actions. Having been incarcerated for mania just one month after the end of the First World War, Charles had absconded from the asylum and soon thereafter had fled to America.

He photographed the entry, saved it to Charles Hughes's family tree profile and immediately emailed it to Edie Loveless with the subject of, *Found it!*

He spent a few minutes more checking that no further records existed for Charles's time in the asylum, then packed up to leave.

Within the ten minutes that Morton had promised Juliette he would be leaving, he was strolling out through reception.

'Bye, Deidre,' Morton called airily to Miss Latimer, knowing that she always hated it when he used her Christian name.

He couldn't fully hear her reply, but he was fairly certain that she'd said, 'Goodbye, Moron.'

He climbed into his Mini, exhaled loudly, then began the forty-five-mile drive back home.

Morton sluggishly walked up the steps to The House with Two Front Doors. Exhaustion was finally creeping over him, and he had not been helped by getting stuck behind a slow tractor crawling half the way across Sussex. He set down his suitcase on the threshold step, put his key in the front door and moved inside. Considering Juliette's obvious annoyance that he had made a slight detour on the way home, the house was surprisingly quiet. He resisted the temptation to take advantage of the rare silence and to go for a lie-down and instead went into the kitchen to make a coffee.

'Welcome home!' came an unexpected chorus of voices as he entered the kitchen.

'You took ages,' Isaac complained, running up to hug him with his sister, Grace.

Juliette hugged them, followed by Margot, then his brother, Jeremy, and brother-in-law, Guy. 'My goodness, I wasn't expecting such a welcoming committee,' Morton said with a grin. 'Thanks, everyone.'

'You need to get in quick with these,' Jeremy said, holding up a take-away box that Morton recognised as coming from his shop, Granny's Scones.

'Yeah, we got fed up waiting,' Juliette said pointedly.

'What flavour are they?' Morton asked, reluctantly taking one from the box.

'Made in honour of your trip,' Guy announced. 'Turkey and pumpkin.'

Morton had to force himself not to ask the myriad of questions in his mind about the two flavours. He noticed Juliette pull a face as he took a bite from the scone. 'Nice,' he lied.

'Well, there's another six left, so tuck in,' Jeremy said.

'So, come on,' Margot said, 'tell us all about the trip. How was Vegas?'

Morton screwed his face up, partly at the question and partly at the taste in his mouth. 'Not really my favourite part of the world. I loved Salt Lake City, though. A genealogist's dream holiday. You wouldn't believe what I found out about your great-grandfather, Juliette. You'll all be delighted to hear that I've got a presentation, all ready to show you.'

Isaac groaned, Grace cheered, and Margot commented, 'Sounds ominous.'

'But first,' Juliette said, 'your children have been working on some things for you. Isaac, do you want to go first?'

'Yes!' he said, hurrying out of the room.

'You need to go with him,' Juliette directed, quietly adding, 'Sorry.'

Morton followed Isaac into the lounge and smiled as his son sat down at the drum kit.

'A song for Daddy,' Isaac announced.

'You wrote a song for me?' Morton asked. 'Fab. Go on, then.'

Needing no further encouragement, Isaac began to hammer out a drum solo that hurt Morton's ears. He maintained a smile throughout the performance, though, touched by the only comprehendible lyrics being, 'I love Daddy.'

Morton clapped enthusiastically when the performance ended. 'That was absolutely amazing,' he said, giving his son a kiss on the head.

Isaac stood up and took a bow. 'Thank you, Daddy.'

Back in the kitchen, Grace handed Morton a stack of papers bound together with two treasury tags. 'What's this?' he asked. On the front cover was a crayon picture of a man holding a gun, standing beside a tree. Above him, in red felt pen were the words *The Adventures of Morton Farrier: Forensic Geologist!*

'It's a story about you, Daddy,' Grace explained. 'Solving

crimes using geology.'

A warm grin spread over Morton's face. He couldn't bring himself to tell her about the confusion between geology and genealogy. 'Do I really need a gun for my job?'

'Mummy said you get yourself into ridiculous and dangerous situations, so I gave you a gun.'

Morton laughed, pulling her into a hug. 'I cannot wait to read it, Graciekins. Thank you.'

'Right, now, sit down and tell us all about your trip,' Margot instructed.

And so he did, being very careful to withhold everything connected with his investigations into Charles Hughes.

Two hours later, with the children in bed and Jeremy and Guy returned home, Morton began to prepare for his presentation. Juliette and Margot were seated in the dark lounge, drinking tea, while he went to fetch his laptop from his bag.

'How long is this going to take?' Margot asked. 'Only, *The One Show* will be on in twenty minutes.'

'Oh, it won't take that long, don't worry,' Morton reassured her.

He opened his laptop, seeing his emails on the screen in front of him. At the top was a message from Edie Loveless thanking him for the image of Charles Hughes's time in the East Sussex County Asylum. Below that were several other unopened emails that could wait until later. But two caught his eye. One was from someone named Brad Jennings with the subject of *New genealogy show!* and the other, which he clicked to open first, was from Duane Reckowski, one of the detectives that Morton had met in Las Vegas. Specifically, the detective who had displayed the least interest in the case. The subject line read, *Your case.*

Hi Morton
It was good to meet you last week and discuss the Candee-Lee Gaddy case.

Upon reviewing the evidence, Detective Marriott and I agree that additional testing of the knife would be appropriate in light of the file of evidence you provided. I can't give you a timeline on this or provide any further information at this time but we will be in touch when we have news.
Regards,
Duane

Morton was elated. Even though it was the outcome that he had been hoping for, it was one he hadn't really been expecting. He didn't want to push the detectives, but he hoped that they would take his advice and run investigative genetic genealogy on the blood sample, certain as he was that it would be found to belong to the late Rosie Hart.

Before he brought up the PowerPoint presentation, Morton quickly clicked on the email from Brad Jennings.

Hi Morton
I work for a TV production company and we're currently setting up a new genealogy show called Celebritrees with one of the major UK TV networks. I watched your genetic genealogy RootsTech presentation and think you could make an excellent host. Give me a call to discuss a screen-test if this is something that interests you. It's a big opportunity and we're negotiating with some pretty big celebrity names for the show.
Best,
Brad

'Oh, my God,' Morton stammered.

'What?' Margot asked, setting down her cup of tea.

'What's happened?' Juliette asked, sounding quite concerned.

'I've just had two unbelievable emails,' he revealed. 'One from the detectives that I met with in Vegas, saying that they will test the blood on the knife and—'

'Wow, that's brilliant news,' Juliette said.

'Yeah, it really is,' Morton agreed. 'And the other email...is from a producer making a new genealogy TV show...and they want me to screen-test for the role of the host.'

Juliette's eyes widened and she leapt up to hug him. 'That's amazing! Oh, my goodness. You'd be fantastic! You've *got* to do it.'

'You were good in that one we watched live,' Margot praised. 'I can just see you, chatting away to Sir Elton John, or Tom Hanks, or Meryl Streep, telling them all about their family tree.'

'I'm not sure,' he countered truthfully.

'You're at least testing for it and that's final,' Juliette said.

'Maybe,' Morton said, looking again at the two emails.

'Can we please get on with this presentation before *The One Show* starts,' Margot asked.

Morton pulled up the presentation. The first slide was a photograph of Charles Hughes beside the title, *The Deserter's Tale.*

Juliette clapped. 'Oh, how exciting.'

As Morton moved through the presentation, he couldn't help but feel a deep, inner calm and happiness spread over his body and mind. Life was good.

Six months later

Epilogue

15th September 2023, Etchingham, East Sussex

Morton climbed out of his Mini, parked up on Etchingham High Street and took in a long breath of the warm air. He was surrounded on all sides by green, open fields. In the near distance was the fourteenth-century parish church, set back from the road behind a low, stone wall. Morton ambled towards it, taking time to enjoy a moment away from a particularly demanding case that he was working on, involving hop-picking and murder in the 1920s.

He arrived at the church, wandered up the main brick path, went around the war memorial, and then began a slow and systematic check of the churchyard. It was well maintained with low-cut grass between an assortment of headstones that wrapped around the ancient building.

Although his current case was a challenging one, it might well be his last for some time, having received the news that he was down to the final two people being considered to host the new TV show, *Celebritrees*. If he got the job and it all went well, then he would likely have to scale back significantly on his genealogical case work.

Moving gradually around to the back of the churchyard, Morton continued to check the names on the gravestones that he passed. He was feeling calm and positive. Since his return from Salt Lake City, things felt as though they were flowing in the correct direction in all areas of his life. Yesterday, he had received an email from the detectives in Las Vegas, saying that the report from Venator, the investigative genetic genealogy company which had tested the blood on the knife that had killed Candee-Lee Gaddy, had arrived. They had given no indication about its content, just that *further investigation was required*. He hoped to goodness that the further investigation would lead to the exoneration of his grandfather, Alfred Farrier. Morton had immediately sent an email to Maddie, simply saying: *Anything to tell me?!?* Hoping that perhaps she might reveal the results of the DNA analysis. Knowing Maddie, though, it was highly unlikely.

In a sunny spot close to the church, Morton found the grave. Crouching down, he read the inscription and then took several photographs.

In Memory of Alice Hughes
A loving mother and grandmother
1892-1969
In spite of everything, a good woman to the end

As with the grave of her estranged husband, the final epithet spoke volumes.

'Life might well have been tough for you, Alice,' Morton said to his great-grandmother-in-law, 'but I think you had a really lucky escape from that man. And, from all accounts, you did a good job of raising the two kids by yourself. Your descendants have done well for themselves; your great-granddaughter is now a serving police inspector.'

He stood for a moment longer, enjoying the sunshine warming his face, then said goodbye to Alice and slowly walked back to his car. He got in and then drove along through the main village, turning left down Oxenbridge Lane. Around fifty yards down the road, Morton pulled over into a lay-by, lowered his window and switched off the engine. On the opposite side of the road was Brookside—a small and quaint cottage covered in a beautiful, red, climbing rose. It had been here that Alice had lived out the majority of her adult life, ostensibly as a single parent. It had been from this house that Charles Hughes had left for the extended duration of the First World War, returning briefly before his incarceration in the East Sussex County

Asylum from where he had then absconded, never to return home again. Was it sentimentality that had made him name his speakeasy after this house? Certainly, the place bore no resemblance whatsoever to Fremont Street in Block 16. Had he ever missed Alice and the children? Had he been truly hounded by whatever horrors that he had seen in the dark days of the war? Or had the allure of vice in the American Wild West been the real driving factor? Morton guessed the answers to those questions were forever consigned to history.

He took out his mobile phone and took a few photographs of Brookside, as requested by Edie Loveless. He opened his emails and sent her the pictures, along with that of Alice Hughes's grave. An unopened email at the top of his inbox attracted his attention. It was from Maddie but with nothing in the subject line. He was certain that it would be her politely declining to reveal the outcome of the investigative genetic genealogy process.

Dear Morton

I'm not sure how you've come to hear about recent developments, but yes, I do have something to tell you.

Back at RootsTech you asked me why I left but I didn't tell you the whole story. A few things have happened recently, and I need to tell you the specific reason that I returned home: I was pregnant.

I appreciate that this will come as a shock. I would have called you, but I don't have your number. Mine is at the bottom of this email if you want to talk.

Maddie

Morton's breath caught in his throat and his right knee gave way for a millisecond.

He re-read the crucial sentence.

Pregnant.

Then, with a crashing clarity in his mind, he remembered

chatting with Maddie's daughter, Jenna, in the lobby of the Kearns Building. She was in her mid-twenties.

Tears ran down his cheeks and he struggled to breathe as a myriad of questions bounced from his heart to his head and back again.

Historical Information

Charles Hughes is loosely based on a real person in my family tree: Charles Dengate, my third cousin three times removed. He also happens to be the great-grandfather of my amazing cover designer, Patrick Dengate.

Although there are lots of similarities between the two men, I have liberally embellished the life of Charles Dengate, an outline of whose real life is detailed below.

Charles Dengate was born in 1890 in London, Ontario, Canada, the son of Alfred Dengate and Sarah Jane Walmsley. Alfred was a native of Northiam in East Sussex (not too far from Morton's home in Rye) but emigrated to Canada as a young man.

The family is shown together in London, Ontario, on the 1891 Canadian Census, where Alfred was working as a baker. After running into trouble with creditors, Alfred, Sarah Jane and their two children, Charles and Clavera, moved across the border into Michigan, USA.

Charles Dengate had an apparently unremarkable childhood. In 1910 he joined the US Navy and trained as an electrician, serving on the U.S.S. Dixie. He was discharged in 1914 and the following year he married Alice Greenhoe. Following the birth of two sons in 1916 and 1917, the family moved to Detroit, where Charles found work as an electrician for Packard Motor Car Company. This job didn't last long, as Charles became gripped by what he later referred to as a 'driving power'. Unlike the trauma that Charles Hughes experienced from the First World War in this story, however, there is no obvious cause for Charles Dengate's subsequent actions.

In October 1919, Charles Dengate failed to come home one evening from his job. The following day, his wife, Alice, went to his employer to find out what had happened to him and was shocked to discover that Charles had not worked there for some time. He had disappeared without a trace and, for the next fifteen years, nobody in the family had any idea where he was or whether he was even still alive.

Letters (including the biblical references) that Charles eventually wrote home—copied, slightly changed and amalgamated in this story—coupled with official documentation, reveal what happened to him after he left home in 1919.

Heading through the American West, Charles had passed through Texas, New Mexico, Arizona, California and Nevada, where he stated that he was always 'pursued by my tormentor.' At one point, he lost everything to gambling, alcohol and prostitutes.

On the 1st September 1926, Charles bigamously married in Glendale, Los Angeles, under the name of George P. Brown. His spouse was a woman named Louise Bullington, a divorcee. The marriage certificate shows the correct names of his parents, with the exception of his father's surname which he changed to Brown to match his own assumed identity.

Around two years after the marriage, Charles abandoned his second wife and found himself in Prescott, Arizona, where he assumed the new name of Roy A. Stewart. There, he met and married Beulah Hennes, a member of the Pentecostal Church, which he also joined. With his new-found faith, Charles stopped smoking, drinking and stealing, and immersed himself in Bible studies. He and Beulah had six children, remaining in the Prescott area for the rest of their lives.

In 1933 and 1938, Charles wrote letters to his first wife, Alice, and their two children, trying to explain what had caused him to leave and offering to return to the marital home. One day in 1938, he did just that. Alice answered the door and apparently fainted on the spot. He was chased away and never returned.

Charles died 16th July 1971 from a cerebral haemorrhage. He was buried in Miracle Valley Cemetery under the name Roy A. Stewart. At the bottom of his headstone is the inscription: *His walk said it all.*

Charles Dengate / George P. Brown / Roy A. Stewart
c.1937

The information presented about the formative years of Las Vegas is correct with the exception of a speakeasy called Brookside, which did not exist.

'Brookside' in Etchingham really exists, although in reality it is actually two pairs of adjoining cottages on Oxenbridge Lane. Number 4 Brookside was actually the home of a different Charles Dengate and his family in the 1920s (the two Charles Dengates were actually fifth cousins once removed).

Acknowledgements

The first person that I would like to thank is my cover designer and sixth cousin, Patrick Dengate. Not only has he created another fantastic cover for this story, but he has also graciously allowed me to base the story of Charles Hughes on his great-grandfather, Charles Dengate. He also shared with me photos and letters written by Charles to his abandoned wife, Alice, and two children, Robert and Maurice, which I used in the story.

Several people appear in this book as themselves, so I would like to offer my sincere gratitude to Else Churchill, Dr Sophie Kay, Diahan Southard, Jonny Perl, Roberta Estes and Drew Smith for so willingly joining Morton on this ten-year-anniversary adventure. For more information about these people, their talks and varied services, please see below:

Else Churchill: sog.org.uk
Dr Sophie Kay: khronicle.co.uk
Diahan Southard: yourdnaguide.com
Jonny Perl: dnapainter.com
Roberta Estes: dna-explained.com

As always, I am indebted to my wonderful group of early readers, who find all manner of missing words, and a few plot holes and lurking errors. Thank you Cheryl Hudson Passey, John Lisle, Pat Richley-Erickson, Lorna Cowan, Natalie Levinson, Helen Smith, Mags Gaulden, Dr Karen Cummings, Elizabeth Swanay O'Neal, Celeste McNeil, Connie Edwards, Laura Wilkinson Hedgecock and Heather Choplin for taking the time to improve the story.

I would like to take this opportunity to thank everyone who has read, reviewed or given positive comments about the series over the last decade; it really is appreciated.

Finally, thanks to my husband, Robert Bristow, for being there from the start of Morton's journey and for accompanying and supporting the adventures ever since. Many of the places Morton visited in this story and the things he got up to we did together in February and March 2023, including almost missing our flight to America because we were eating and drinking too much in the airport lounge and, yes, both doing genealogy.

Further Information

Website & Newsletter: www.nathandylangoodwin.com
BlueSky: @NathanDylanGoodwin
Facebook: www.facebook.com/NathanDylanGoodwin
Pinterest: www.pinterest.com/NathanDylanGoodwin
Instagram: www.instagram.com/NathanDylanGoodwin
LinkedIn: www.linkedin.com/in/NathanDylanGoodwin

Hiding the Past
(The Forensic Genealogist #1)

Peter Coldrick had no past; that was the conclusion drawn by years of personal and professional research. Then he employed the services of one Morton Farrier, Forensic Genealogist – a stubborn, determined man who uses whatever means necessary to uncover the past. With the Coldrick Case, Morton faces his toughest and most dangerous assignment yet, where all of his investigative and genealogical skills are put to the test. However, others are also interested in the Coldrick family, people who will stop at nothing, including murder, to hide the past. As Morton begins to unearth his client's mysterious past, he is forced to confront his own family's dark history, a history which he knows little about.

'Flicking between the present and stories and extracts from the past, the pace never lets up in an excellent addition to this unique genre of literature'
Your Family Tree magazine

'At times amusing and shocking, this is a fast-moving modern crime mystery with genealogical twists. The blend of well fleshed-out characters, complete with flaws and foibles, will keep you guessing until the end'
Family Tree magazine

The Lost Ancestor
(The Forensic Genealogist #2)

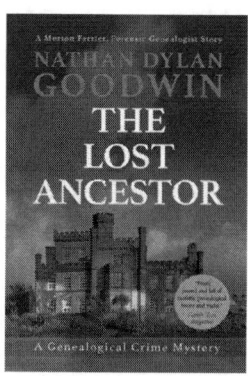

When Morton Farrier, the formidable forensic genealogist, is called upon to uncover the mysterious disappearance of a housemaid working in a large Edwardian country house in 1911, he embarks on a perilous journey into the past. Uncovering surprising secrets and facing dangerous adversaries, Morton must use his comprehensive genealogical skills to solve the case. Will he be able to put the pieces together before it's too late?

'If you enjoy a novel with a keen eye for historical detail, solid writing, believable settings and a sturdy protagonist, *The Lost Ancestor* is a safe bet. Here British author Nathan Dylan Goodwin spins a riveting genealogical crime mystery with a pulsing, realistic storyline'
Your Family Tree magazine

'Finely paced and full of realistic genealogical terms and tricks, this is an enjoyable whodunit with engaging research twists that keep you guessing until the end. If you enjoy genealogical fiction and Ruth Rendell mysteries, you'll find this a pleasing page-turner'
Family Tree magazine

The Orange Lilies
(The Forensic Genealogist #3)

Morton Farrier has spent his entire career as a forensic genealogist solving other people's family history secrets, all the while knowing so little of his very own family's mysterious past. However, this poignant Christmastime novella sees Morton's skills put to use much closer to home, as he must confront his own past, present and future through events both present-day and one hundred years ago. It seems that not every soldier saw a truce on the Western Front that 1914 Christmas…

'The Orange Lilies sees Morton for once investigating his own tree (and about time too!). Moving smoothly between Christmas 1914 and Christmas 2014, the author weaves an intriguing tale with more than a few twists - several times I thought I'd figured it all out, but each time there was a surprise waiting in the next chapter… Thoroughly recommended - and I can't wait for the next novel'
LostCousins

'Morton confronts a long-standing mystery in his own family— one that leads him just a little closer to the truth about his personal origins. This Christmas-time tale flashes back to Christmas 1914, to a turning point in his relatives' lives. Don't miss it!'
Lisa Louise Cooke

The America Ground
(The Forensic Genealogist #4)

Morton Farrier, the esteemed English forensic genealogist, had cleared a space in his busy schedule to track down his own elusive father finally. But he is then presented with a case that challenges his research skills in his quest to find the killer of a woman murdered more than one hundred and eighty years ago. Thoughts of his own family history are quickly and violently pushed to one side as Morton rushes to complete his investigation before other sinister elements succeed in derailing the case.

'As in the earlier novels, each chapter slips smoothly from past to present, revealing murderous events as the likeable Morton uncovers evidence in the present, while trying to solve the mystery of his own paternity. Packed once more with glorious detail of records familiar to family historians, *The America Ground* is a delightfully pacey read'
Family Tree magazine

'Like most genealogical mysteries this book has several threads, cleverly woven together by the author - and there are plenty of surprises for the reader as the story approaches its conclusion. A jolly good read!'
LostCousins

The Spyglass File
(The Forensic Genealogist #5)

Morton Farrier was no longer at the top of his game. His forensic genealogy career was faltering and he was refusing to accept any new cases, preferring instead to concentrate on locating his own elusive biological father. Yet, when a particular case presents itself, that of finding the family of a woman abandoned in the midst of the Battle of Britain, Morton is compelled to help her to unravel her past. Using all of his genealogical skills, he soon discovers that the case is connected to The Spyglass File*—a secretive document which throws up links which threaten to disturb the wrongdoings of others, who would rather its contents, as well as their actions, remain hidden forever.*

'If you like a good mystery, and the detective work of genealogy, this is another mystery novel from Nathan which will have you whizzing through the pages with time slipping by unnoticed'
Your Family History magazine

'The first page was so overwhelming that I had to stop for breath...Well, the rest of the book certainly lived up to that impressive start, with twists and turns that kept me guessing right to the end... As the story neared its conclusion I found myself conflicted, for much as I wanted to know how Morton's assignment panned out, I was enjoying it so much that I really didn't want this book to end!'
LostCousins

The Missing Man
(The Forensic Genealogist #6)

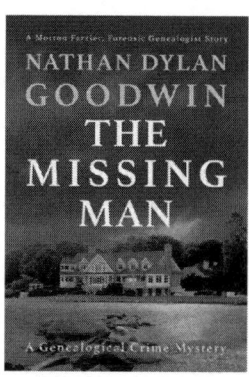

It was to be the most important case of Morton Farrier's career in forensic genealogy so far. A case that had eluded him for many years: finding his own father. Harley 'Jack' Jacklin disappeared just six days after a fatal fire at his Cape Cod home on Christmas Eve in 1976, leaving no trace behind. Now his son, Morton must travel to the East Coast of America to unravel the family's dark secrets in order to discover what really happened to him.

'One of the hallmarks of genealogical mystery novels is the way that they weave together multiple threads and this book is no exception, cleverly skipping across the generations - and there's also a pleasing symmetry that helps to endear us to one of the key characters...If you've read the other books in this series you won't need me to tell you to rush out and buy this one'
LostCousins

'Nathan Dylan Goodwin has delivered another page-turning mystery laden with forensic genealogical clues that will keep any family historian glued to the book until the mystery is solved'
Eastman's Online Genealogy Newsletter

The Suffragette's Secret
(A Forensic Genealogist short story)

Morton Farrier's life has been turned upside down by the recent addition to his household. Despite his perpetual exhaustion, he is determined to crack his latest genealogical investigation: the mystery of one Grace Emmerson, a militant suffragette, who also happens to be his wife's great-grandmother. Using a range of genealogical skills and resources, Morton sets out to discover Grace's secret past.

'Everyone should read this story of courage'
Genealogical Society of the Northern Territory

'What a story!'
LostCousins

'Goodwin's writing brings the events and the people into interesting focus. Fascinating background for readers who might be unfamiliar with this history'
Queensland Family History Society

The Wicked Trade
(The Forensic Genealogist #7)

When Morton Farrier is presented with a case revolving around a mysterious letter written by disreputable criminal, Ann Fothergill in 1827, he quickly finds himself delving into a shadowy Georgian underworld of smuggling and murder on the Kent and Sussex border. Morton must use his skills as a forensic genealogist to untangle Ann's association with the notorious Aldington Gang and also with the brutal killing of Quartermaster Richard Morgan. As his research continues, Morton suspects that his client's family might have more troubling and dangerous expectations of his findings.

'Once again the author has carefully built the story around real places, real people, and historical facts - and whilst the tale itself is fictional, it's so well written that you'd be forgiven for thinking it was true'
LostCousins

'I can thoroughly recommend this book, which is a superior example of its genre. It is an ideal purchase for anyone with an interest in reading thrillers and in family history studies. I look forward to the next instalment of Morton Farrier's quest!'
Waltham Forest FHS

The Sterling Affair
(The Forensic Genealogist #8)

When an unannounced stranger comes calling at Morton Farrier's front door, he finds himself faced with the most intriguing and confounding case of his career to-date as a forensic genealogist. He agrees to accept the contract to identify a man who had been secretly living under the name of his new client's long-deceased brother. Morton must use his range of resources and research skills to help him deconstruct this mysterious man's life, ultimately leading him back into the murky world of 1950s international affairs of state. Meanwhile, Morton is faced with his own alarmingly close DNA match which itself comes with far-reaching implications for the Farriers.

'If you love a whodunnit, *The Sterling Affair* is sure to grab your curiosity, and if you enjoy family history, you'll relish the read all the more'
Family History magazine

'The events of the book are as much of a roller-coaster ride for Morton as they are for the reader. If you're an avid reader of Nathan Dylan Goodwin's books you won't need to be convinced to buy this latest instalment in the Forensic Genealogist series - but if you're not, now's the time to start, because *The Sterling Affair* is a real cracker!'
LostCousins

The Foundlings
(The Forensic Genealogist #9)

Forensic genealogist, Morton Farrier, agrees to take on a case to identify the biological mother of three foundlings, abandoned in shop doorways as new-born babies in the 1970s. He has just one thing with which to begin his investigation: the three women's DNA, one of whom is his half-aunt. With just six days of research time available to him, his investigation uncovers some shocking revelations and troubling links to his own grandfather; and Morton finds that, for the first time in his career, he is advising his clients not to read his concluding report.

'This is a fun and engaging read that will transport you back to a memorable decade'
Family Tree magazine

'This is one of the best books in an excellent series...Highly recommended'
LostCousins

'Absolutely riveting — the best yet in this series!'
Tacoma-Pierce County Genealogical Society

'A must read for anyone who loves unraveling genealogy mysteries'
Columbia County Historical & Genealogical Society

The Deserter's Tale
(The Forensic Genealogist #10)

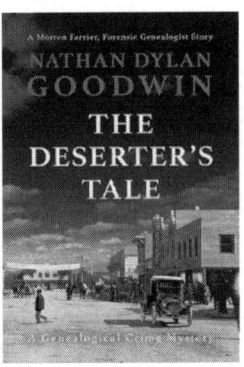

When forensic genealogist Morton Farrier accepted an invitation to travel to Salt Lake City, Utah, to speak at the RootsTech genealogy conference, he had been unaware that one of his co-panellists was to be none other than his former girlfriend, Madison Scott-Barnhart. Whilst he prepares anxiously to meet her for what will be the first time in twenty-six years—and hopefully to discover the unresolved truth behind her abrupt ending of their relationship—he takes on the case of researching his wife's mysterious great-grandfather: a man who deserted his Sussex family shortly after the First World War. In the course of his investigations and time in the States, Morton uncovers some shocking truths, some of which are uncomfortably close to home…

'Well written and easy to read, believable characters, plot twists and turns and with real genealogical research at the heart of each story'
Hertfordshire Family History Society

'You won't be disappointed!'
LostCousins

'The writing is easy and fast paced, intriguing, mysterious, and often humorous. Every genealogy researcher can relate to the great research tips and methodology that the author describes'
The London Leaf

Printed in Dunstable, United Kingdom

73707268R00087